"You do take proper, um, precautions, don't you?"

At her question, James's blue eyes narrowed skeptically. "Why, do you have plans for after dinner?"

Kelly stared at her plate. "No, I—I was just making conversation."

"Lady, either you make unusual conversation, or you had an ulterior motive in asking me to dinner." He grinned. "Not too many first dates ask me about hereditary diseases."

Kelly snuck a glance at him from under her lashes, and her heart sank. Could she go through with it?

"James," she started, "I have to be honest with you. I did have a purpose for asking you out...."

He stiffened slightly. "Well?"

"I wanted to get to know you—" Kelly drew a deep breath "—and to ask you to be the father of my baby."

ABOUT THE AUTHOR

Judy Christenberry wrote Regency romances
for twelve years—part of the time for Harlequin
Regency as Judith Stafford—before writing
this, her first American Romance novel. She
lives in Plano, Texas, with her two daughters,
where she still teaches high school French. A
baseball fanatic, Judy follows the Texas Rangers
whenever she finds time. Her advice to aspiring
writers: "Don't wait around for it to happen—
make it happen!"

Judy Christenberry

FINDING DADDY

Harlequin Books

TORONTO • NEW YORK • LONDON
AMSTERDAM • PARIS • SYDNEY • HAMBURG
STOCKHOLM • ATHENS • TOKYO • MILAN
MADRID • WARSAW • BUDAPEST • AUCKLAND

To Barbara Bretton,
for her incredible generosity and encouragement

ISBN 0-373-16555-2

FINDING DADDY

Chapter One

Intelligence?

Well, of course, that was essential.

And courage. He didn't have to rescue damsels in distress, but he had to at least have the courage of his convictions.

Kelly Abbott nibbled on her bottom lip as she studied her list. What next? A sense of humor. Yes, she wanted someone who could laugh at himself as well as others.

She closed her eyes as she remembered the laughter and teasing she'd shared with her grandfather. He'd taught her to laugh when she goofed, then to pick herself up and carry on.

And that's what she would do now. Carry on. She feared she'd need laughter to get through the task she'd set for herself. Her mind skittered away from thinking about what was to come.

Compassion? Without compassion, he—whoever she chose—wouldn't be able to understand why. She added that word to her list. His understanding would be necessary.

Her thoughts were drawn to a second list she'd already made. With a sigh, she let her gaze run down the names. One seemed to jump out at her every time she saw it.

James Townsend.

Why did the man's name draw such a reaction from her? she wondered, even as a shudder shot down her spine. She scarcely knew him.

He was a client of her advertising agency where she'd worked for seven years, but she hadn't had a lot of contact with him. Lately, though, she'd run into him several times at the office. The last time he'd continued to watch her as she'd walked away. She'd known because his blue-eyed gaze had sent chills all over her body.

She couldn't explain her reaction. There were others more handsome, younger, a few more successful, though not many. No, there was no logical explanation. Yet she'd hesitated to add him to her list.

The fluttering panic that filled her stomach whenever she thought of him warned her that choosing James Townsend would complicate her carefully made plans. She'd put him on her list, but not first. No, definitely not first.

Time to get back to what she was looking for, she vowed, shoving aside thoughts of James Townsend. Athletic? She didn't need a Michael Jordan, but someone with coordination, good health and a good body, for her own satisfaction. Without warning, her mind conjured images of James Townsend in his conservative business suits.

"Get the man out of your head, Kelly!" she told herself in irritation. She needed a man who met her requirements, of course. But she also needed someone who didn't interest her.

And that was the one qualification James Townsend failed. Dennis Crane might do. He was a successful lawyer. And Richard Burley. She hadn't seen him in a few months, but he was ... pleasant. And Bobby Sholds. He met a lot of the necessary qualifications. And didn't raise her blood pressure.

She needed to remain calm. Time was running out. She wouldn't—couldn't—fail. After all, she'd promised Granddad.

So, how to go about it?

She chewed on the eraser of her pencil. Then, with deliberate slowness, she wrote a number by each name. With a sigh, the last number went to James Townsend.

"It's probably the only time he's come in last," she muttered. With luck, she'd find the perfect candidate for her plan before she ever got to his name. Her desperate plan.

There hadn't been anyone to turn to for advice. With each passing day, she'd grown more worried, unable to share her fears. Only her plan had given her a glimmer of hope.

Now, if she could just carry it out. Her promise to her grandfather as he lay dying said she could. Her fear insisted she should. Her hope demanded she must. ⁓

She turned back to her lists.

"I'M SO GLAD I RAN into you Monday, Bobby," Kelly said, smiling at the handsome man across from her. He had no idea what stratagems she'd resorted to to create that casual meeting.

"Me, too, Kelly, baby. Long time no see."

Beneath her smile, Kelly grimaced. She hated being called baby. "So, what are you doing these days?"

"Oh, this and that. I've got a big deal working right now. Hush, hush, so I can't tell you about it, but when everything breaks just right, I'll be sittin' pretty."

Another two hours of listening to Bobby's pipe dreams convinced Kelly to cross him off her list. *She* wouldn't have any interest in living if she had to spend much more time with him.

She'd left out the importance of personality. Maybe such a trait was learned, not inherited, but she wasn't willing to take that risk. Besides, with Bobby, she'd fall asleep before she could accomplish her goal. *You wouldn't be bored with James Townsend,* a little voice whispered. She ignored it.

Her shoulders were slumped and her lips drooping as she crossed the threshold of her bedroom, but she didn't give herself any slack. She couldn't quit now after having only tried one man.

She immediately crossed to the desk and picked up the list she'd made only a couple of nights ago. The next name on the paper was Richard Burley. She'd call him tomorrow. He was an intelligent man, so he already was ahead of Bobby. Maybe he'd be the one.

SO FAR SO GOOD. Richard was pleasant company. He had talked about any number of interesting things. Time to get more personal.

"Richard, why haven't you married?" An impertinent question, but one women always had to put up with. So why not him? She held her breath for his reply.

"Actually, I have, but it's not a happy marriage. She doesn't understand me. Why, you wouldn't believe—"

Cross Richard off the list.

"DENNIS, how's your legal practice doing?"

"Quite well, Kelly. Need a loan?"

Kelly's cheeks flamed, but she smiled at her dinner companion. "No, Dennis, I'm doing fine, myself. I just wondered if you liked your work."

"Hell, yes, I like my work. I'm raking in the bucks hand over fist. Say, have you seen my commercial? The one late at night? I'm outdoing the lawyer who says he sends flowers. I send flowers *and* candy, so all those accident victims will let *me* sue the other guy." He grinned, and Kelly hoped it was her imagination that made his teeth look like they'd been filed to sharp points.

"Don't you handle other kinds of cases?"

"Not anymore. I use to do some divorce work, but that's always messy. And you don't make nearly as much money. Why, I get up in front of that jury, and I just pour it on. I have my client slump down in his chair, looking as pitiful as he can, and I just wring their hearts."

He sounded so pleased with himself, Kelly didn't bother to express her disapproval. She just crossed him off her list.

SHE STARED at the now-rumpled piece of paper. Every name but one had a heavy black line through it. James Townsend. She wavered, wondering if she should give up on her plan—or at least this version of it.

But she'd already wasted so much time on the other men on her list. One more night and the decision would be out of her hands.

Besides, it would finally prove to herself that she wasn't a coward.

"I'M GLAD YOU COULD join me, James." She smiled fleetingly at the man across from her, then looked away. He was too attractive for his own good. Not picture-book handsome, but rugged, strong, self-assured.

"My pleasure, Kelly. It's not often a beautiful woman asks me to dinner."

She didn't believe that for a minute. Every woman in the restaurant had taken a long hungry look at him when they'd entered.

"Are you pleased with the work we've done for you?" she asked, desperately searching for a neutral topic of conversation.

"Don't tell me Tex put you up to this? And here I thought you were interested in *me*." He pretended disappointment, but his eyes were sparkling with laughter.

Dark blue eyes. With little laugh wrinkles at the corners.

"No, of course not," she hurriedly assured him. "Tex is too straightforward to do any such thing. I guess I was just searching for something to talk about."

"Why don't we talk about you?"

"Me? That would be a little boring."

"I don't think so. How long have you worked at Bauer, Tate & Warner?"

As Kelly talked about her job at the agency, the waiter arrived to take their orders. James waited quietly as she made her choice. And he didn't try to make the decision for her.

One requirement down, she thought. He had patience.

They continued to talk after the waiter left.

"I live with my grandmother," she said, in response to a question. "I know I'm a little old to still be living at home, but I'm comfortable there, and I don't want to leave Gran alone."

She watched him carefully for his response.

"If you're both happy with the situation, I don't see what anyone else thinks should matter."

Understanding, too.

"Do you like old people?"

He blinked before answering. "I don't have anything against them. I even have two for parents. They qualify, don't they?" The teasing glint in his eyes brought a smile to Kelly's lips.

Three for three, she commented to herself. *He's even got a sense of humor.*

"Not if they're within hearing distance."

"Ah. Smart lady. No, they retired to Arizona."

"Are you close to them?"

"I visit them several times a year and occasionally they come back to Dallas. My mother says the shopping in Dallas can't be beat."

"Do you shop with her?"

James leaned back in his chair, grinning. "Not on your life. I'd be the one feeling old by the end of the day."

"Do your parents ever press you about having grandchildren?" She held her breath, hoping he wouldn't think her question was too personal.

He studied her without answering, and she wondered if those dark blue eyes could see right into her mind.

"They'd rather I get married first."

Before she could pursue the subject, the waiter returned with their meals. She let him take several bites before she returned to her questioning.

"But you were married once."

"Yes." He put his fork down and looked at her. "You've certainly done your homework, haven't you?" Suddenly, he seemed more withdrawn, not the friendly person she'd just been talking to.

"Is your marriage a secret? I'm sorry. Someone at work must have mentioned it, and I didn't think it would bother you." She drew a calming breath and then asked an even more personal question.

"Are you still in love with her?"

"No."

There was no emotion in his voice, but Kelly knew she'd upset him. She gave him a friendly smile. "I just wondered, because before my grandfather died, the two of them, he and Gran, used to tease me about having their great-grandchild."

He paused to take a bite of his steak before saying, "I think my parents don't mention grandchildren because they don't want to upset me. Besides, they have my sister's two kids."

"So you're not interested in having children?"

"I wouldn't say that. It's just that a child wouldn't fit into my life-style right now."

Perfect.

She allowed the conversation to drift into impersonal subjects for a while.

After they'd discussed the ins and outs of business in Dallas, she said, "You must play some kind of sports to keep in such good condition."

He shrugged, which only emphasized the breadth of his shoulders. "Nothing organized. I like handball, pick-up basketball, things like that. And I do a little jogging."

She sat there lost in thought. Damn, she couldn't find anything wrong with him. Why couldn't he have some glaring fault that would allow her to dismiss him?

"Kelly? Are you still with me?"

"Oh, yes, sorry. Do you drink?"

His lips slipped into a sideways grin she found enormously attractive. "That's kind of a *non sequitur,* isn't it?"

Flustered, she searched for a connection. "Not really, if you think about it. I doubt any great athletes are heavy drinkers."

"You've got me there," he agreed. "However, I don't pretend to be a great athlete."

She said nothing, wondering how to rephrase her question, but he continued, much to her relief. "I also am not much of a drinker. An occasional glass of wine is my limit."

"That's good because—because drinkers tend to have a lot of other diseases, don't you think?"

He was giving her a strange look, but he nodded in agreement. "Yes, I suppose so."

"Some diseases are hereditary, of course. I had an aunt who contracted cancer." He nodded again. She forced herself to go on. "Does your family have any history of diseases?"

"Not that I know of, but if you want the name of my family doctor, I can give it to you." Though he was still smiling, Kelly thought the smile had lost some of its warmth. Maybe he'd make the decision for her and refuse to go out with her again because he wondered about her sanity. She was beginning to wonder about it, too.

One last subject had to be covered and she gulped her ice tea before she launched into her next topic.

"No, I don't need your doctor's name," she said with what she hoped was a casual laugh. "Though dating in the nineties does involve a few complications."

He gave her a blank look and she fought to keep her groan silent. He wasn't going to give her any help on this one. "I mean, with AIDS and all."

His blue eyes remained narrowed as he stared at her.

"You—you do take proper precautions, don't you?"

"You have plans for after dinner?" James asked in a carefully controlled voice.

She thought she'd curl into a tiny ball and sink beneath the table in embarrassment. Instead, she sipped more tea before returning the glass to its place on the table, her fingers only slightly trembling.

"No, that wasn't what I—I was trying to say."

"No?"

"No! I was just making conversation."

He continued to stare at her, but she kept her gaze glued to her plate. Finally he said, "Kelly, either you have an unusual style of conversation, unlike anyone I've ever met, or there's a purpose behind your questions."

Her cheeks flamed. "W-what do you mean?"

"I wish I knew. I thought we were going to talk about you, but instead I've been answering some pretty bizarre questions."

"Bizarre?" She felt like a parrot, repeating his words, but he'd taken her by surprise.

"Not too many first dates ask me about hereditary diseases in my family."

"Oh." *That question had been a mistake.*

"Nor do they want to know if my parents are longing for grandchildren."

"I was just making conversation," she said defensively, looking away.

"I shouldn't think a woman as beautiful and intelligent as you would have to work at it so much."

He leaned across the table and picked up her hand, his fingers caressing hers. "In fact, a woman as beautiful as you probably doesn't have to ask a man to take her out."

"Haven't you heard of women's lib?" she asked, her chin rising. "There's nothing wrong with my asking a man out if I want to."

He grinned. "I didn't say there was. I just said I was surprised that you did. All you had to do was flirt with me a little and I would've done the asking. Why didn't you?''

''Flirt with you? Well—well, I hadn't seen you in a couple of months. And I'm a straightforward person.''

''Like Tex,'' he said, that teasing look in his eyes again as he mentioned her boss. Her obvious discomfort with their conversation seemed to have relaxed him. He released her hand and sat back in his chair. ''So, you had no ulterior motives in asking me out?''

''Not—not exactly,'' she murmured, staring at her scarcely touched food.

''Well, that's certainly cleared everything up,'' he muttered. She snuck a quick glance at him from under her eyelashes, and her heart sank as she saw the skeptical look on his face.

Could she go through with it?

Gran's wan face flashed into her head. Yes. Yes, she could, but she didn't think she could do so in a public place.

''Look, James, I asked you out for a reason, but I'd rather not talk about it here. Could we wait until later, when we're alone?''

''In the car? Are we going parking, like a couple of teenagers? I'm a little long in the tooth for such cramped quarters, Kelly.''

Her entire face flooded with color. ''James! That's not what— Oh, never mind!''

''Sorry,'' he said, but Kelly didn't see any remorse in his grin.

Anger gave her the courage she'd earlier lacked. With her chin up, she said, "I was wrong not to have been honest with you from the first. I did have a purpose in asking you out."

His gaze narrowed and he stiffened slightly. "Well?"

"I asked you out to—to get to know you, of course, and—" she paused and drew a deep breath "—and to ask you to be the father of my baby."

Chapter Two

James Townsend gasped for air and then swallowed too much. His coughing fit drew the gaze of everyone in the restaurant.

After he'd thanked the hovering waiter and assured him he would survive, James turned a wary eye toward his dinner companion. "Did you say what I think you said?"

"Yes, but—"

"That's why you asked me out?"

"Yes, but—"

"Don't you think you're expecting a lot on the first date?" he asked, his words laced with sarcasm.

"James! Would you let me finish a sentence?"

"I'm not sure it's safe after the last sentence you finished." He couldn't help enjoying the flush that filled her cheeks, even as he was appalled by the topic of their conversation.

Kelly Abbott was a delightful dinner companion. In fact, James had been pleased by her call. He'd been attracted to her from the first time they met at her office, but he hadn't initiated any contact because she always seemed more a home-and-hearth woman than someone just out for fun. After his disastrous marriage, he steered away from any serious relationships. Her call had made him think she'd changed her mind. Her question told him she hadn't.

"I didn't mean to shock you. And if you'll let me explain, I'm sure you'll agree that—that my request is reasonable."

"I'd like to bet the ranch on that one," he muttered under his breath.

"What?"

"Nothing. I can't wait to hear your explanation."

In fact, he dreaded it. His history with women wasn't the best. His marriage had failed when he found his wife in bed with another man. Since then, he'd sought only temporary liaisons, not wanting to trust any woman enough to marry her.

That hadn't stopped women from targeting him as a marriage prospect. After all, he wasn't repulsive, and the manufacturing company he owned was quite successful. Several women had suggested marriage. Another had simply told him she was pregnant, even though he'd taken every precaution. He'd agreed to do the honorable thing—the moment a blood test proved the child was his. She'd disappeared.

He hadn't wanted to believe Kelly Abbott was like the others.

Now she was about to prove him right about not being able to trust women.

With his thoughts in turmoil, it took several minutes to realize she hadn't responded to his encouragement to explain. "Change your mind?"

"No. But I don't think I can explain here, in public."

His eyebrows soared. "And what kind of explanation do you intend that requires privacy?"

"Not what you're thinking, obviously!" she snapped.

He hadn't even recognized the faint hope that had been growing in him until it had been smashed. The hope that Kelly Abbott was different. It irritated him. He thought he'd stamped out such naive yearnings.

He wiped his mouth with his napkin and laid the cloth on the table. "Look, Kelly, I've enjoyed your company, but nothing else is in the cards. I told you a child wouldn't fit into my life-style right now."

"I know. That's why you're perfect."

Was she completely off her rocker? Nothing was making sense, and he didn't think the problem was with him. "Kelly, you can't—"

"Please, give me a chance to explain. If you say no after I explain, we'll forget this conversation ever took place."

Fat chance! He studied Kelly, her auburn hair and green eyes a striking combination. She was a beauty, but even more, she was an intelligent, interesting woman. Why would she suggest such a thing? And then tell him he was perfect because he didn't want a child?

"All right. Where?"

"I—we can't go home because I don't want Gran— That is, it would be difficult to be private."

"My place?" Was he walking into a trap? She was above the legal age, so he thought he was safe.

"If you don't mind."

When he only nodded, she signaled the waiter who sped to their table at once.

"Yes, ma'am?"

"We're finished," she said, delicately gesturing to their plates.

"There was something wrong with your dinner?"

James realized his steak was half-finished. Somehow he'd lost interest in such a mundane thing as eating. "Everything was fine. I guess we didn't have much of an appetite."

"We have some desserts that will tempt you. Shall I bring the dessert tray?" The waiter used his most winning smile.

After a glance at James for confirmation, which he quickly gave, Kelly said no and asked for the check. The disappointed waiter turned away, and she reached for her purse.

"My treat, Kelly," James quickly said, putting his hand on her arm.

"No. I invited you, James."

He would've liked to have argued. Somehow it would have made him feel more in control. The evening hadn't gone according to his expectations. But he let her pay the bill the waiter presented only a minute later.

As soon as she'd signed the charge slip, he stood and pulled back her chair for her. Her smile of thanks was minimal, as if she had something else on her mind.

He had met her at the restaurant, so they got into separate cars and he led the way back to his condominium. While he drove, James reviewed the conversation at the restaurant.

In a way, he guessed he should be grateful she'd said what she did. Otherwise, he might have found himself doing the one thing he'd promised he'd never do: fall for another woman. The spell Kelly cast with her beauty, her wit, her warmth, was powerful.

Now he could relegate her to the women in his past, those who had lied to him, tricked him, tried to take him for his money. It was safer that way. Too bad.

After they parked their cars, he escorted her to the elevator and inserted his key to take them to the penthouse. When the door opened to the top floor, he said, "Make yourself at home, Kelly. May I get you something to drink?"

"No—no, thank you." She stepped into his living room, her gaze traveling around the area.

He wondered what she thought of his home. He'd had one of the best decorators in Dallas redo his penthouse last year. The result was sophisticated perfection—a lot of white touched by acid yellow and green— and a magnificent view of the Dallas skyline.

She walked toward the floor-to-ceiling windows.

"You like the view?" he asked, following her.

"It's wonderful. You must enjoy living here."

He shrugged. It was sufficient for his needs.

She turned from the windows, and he noticed her clenched fingers and trembling bottom lip.

"Come sit down and relax. I want to hear your explanation."

She chose one of the overstuffed chairs, ignoring the two white sofas. He sat down, also, but she said nothing.

"Look, I know about the ticking clock syndrome. Is that what your having a baby is about? Because I have to tell you I think you have a few good years left." His teasing had no effect on her at all, unless it was to bite her bottom lip. He'd noted that habit during the evening, and it drove him to distraction. Her lips were full and soft, spreading to a beautiful smile. Every movement invited his touch.

"Kelly?"

She turned to look at him. "I may have a few years left, James, but my grandmother doesn't." Tears filled her eyes, and she hurriedly looked away.

Puzzled, he stared at her. "I don't understand."

"I—I need to have a child for my grandmother."

Her quiet words seemed to echo off the glass of the windows. As one lone tear trickled down her pale cheek, he rose from the sofa and knelt beside her chair.

"Honey, I don't know what your grandmother has said to you, but this decision should be yours. The best reason, the only reason, to have a child is because you and the man you love want one.''

He tenderly wiped the moisture from her skin and found himself leaning toward her, as if he couldn't resist touching those trembling lips with his.

She pulled back, snapping him from her spell. ''No. I'm not explaining this well. My grandmother doesn't know.''

Leaning back on his heels, he made an effort to concentrate on her words. ''Then why did you say the baby was for your grandmother?''

She rose from her chair and walked a few steps away from him. He stood, wondering if she was going to leave without explaining.

''My grandfather died almost four months ago.''

James moved closer to her, barely able to hear her whisper.

''He and my grandmother had been married fifty-four years. They were inseparable.'' She swung around to face him. ''My grandmother is dying of a broken heart.''

James opened his mouth to protest her words, but she forestalled him. ''Don't tell me that's not possible. Even the doctor has come to the same conclusion.''

''Maybe you need to see a new doctor.''

''Do you think I haven't tried?'' Kelly cried out in anguish. ''I've taken her to so many doctors, she says she's become a pincushion and refuses to go again!''

James chuckled. ''She sounds pretty good to me.''

''It's not funny!'' she protested, her voice cracking.

With a quick step, he reached out and drew her trembling body against his. Only to comfort her, he assured himself. He'd be a jerk to think of anything else right now.

"Come on, Kelly, you know I wasn't laughing at your grandmother's illness. Just take it easy."

She leaned against him like a tired child, as if the strain had been too much. He guided her to one of the sofas and sat down, keeping her in the circle of his arm.

"Explain why a baby is so important."

Drawing a deep breath, as if to compose herself, Kelly sat stiffly beside him. "A baby will make her feel needed."

"That's it? Can't you make her feel needed some other way?"

"I've tried. You don't understand."

"No," he agreed with a frown, "but I'm trying to. It seems to me you need a lot better reason than that for bringing a child into the world."

"Half the babies in the world are accidents. At least I have a reason," she said tightly. "Look, I'm independent. I always have been. Financially I have no problems. My grandfather and both parents left me trust funds. Gran sees right through me whenever I try to act helpless."

"So how did you come up with the idea of the baby?" he asked, distracted by the strands of silky hair playing through his fingers on the back of the sofa.

"A great-grandchild is the only thing she's shown any interest in. I told you she and Granddad always teased me about the importance of the next generation."

"So why don't you find a nice guy, marry him and set up housekeeping?" he suggested lightly, his gaze roving over her. In spite of his own determination never to remarry, he couldn't help feeling envious of whomever she chose.

Kelly jumped up from the sofa and strode back to the windows, her arms wrapped around her body. "I have no intention of marrying." Her voice was cold, forbidding.

"A child needs both parents."

"Too bad someone didn't tell my father that," she drawled, turning to stare at him. "Or half the other fathers in the world who abandon their children. At least my child would have one loving parent with the means to support it."

He stared at her, unable to deny her statement, but he still couldn't agree with her. "There must be another way to help your grandmother, Kelly. Having a baby isn't a good idea."

FRUSTRATION ROSE IN KELLY as she stared at the perfect father for her child. Why did he have to have a conscience? She was offering him what most men set out to win on a date, and he was turning her down.

"You said it should be my decision. It is. All I'm asking for is a little cooperation." She gave him her best smile.

Even though he returned her smile, he shook his head. "I told you earlier, a baby wouldn't fit in my life right now. And I have no intention of marrying, even though your offer is tempting."

Kelly realized she'd left out an essential part of her explanation. Maybe it would change his mind. "That's why you're perfect."

"You said something like that before, but it doesn't make sense."

"I don't want you to have a baby in *your* life. And if you'll think back, you'll remember I never mentioned marriage." She stared at him triumphantly, hoping to see a change in his attitude.

There was a change, all right. He leapt from the sofa, a ferocious frown on his face. "Let me get this straight. You want me to father your child and then pretend neither of you exists?"

"Exactly," she exclaimed, relieved that he finally understood.

"Why in the hell would I want to do that?"

He might understand, but he didn't appear happy about it. When he took several steps toward her, she backed away.

"I didn't think about it as an actual choice on your part," she said, trying to sound reasonable. "I need a little cooperation from you, that's all. I mean, a lot of men *expect* a woman to go to bed with them on the first date, for heaven's sake!"

"A lot of men are jerks!"

"I won't argue with you there!" she returned with just as much heat. They glared at each other until she saw a twinkle of laughter appear in his eyes.

"I think I just insulted my half of the human race."

She let herself relax a little. "I believe you did."

He extended a hand. "Let's sit down and try again before I say something *else* I shouldn't."

Reluctantly, she placed her hand in his and let him lead her back to the sofa. She'd already discovered, when he'd comforted her earlier, that touching him was not a good idea. She liked it too much.

He rubbed his thumb over her knuckles, keeping his gaze on her hand. "Kelly, I couldn't father a child and walk away. That wouldn't be right."

"But, James, I don't need any financial support. I've already told you that. I'd be glad to sign papers promising not to ask for money... or marriage." She leaned toward him, pleading with her body as much as her words.

He groaned. "Don't look at me like that."

She sank her teeth into her bottom lip and straightened.

Jumping from the sofa, he strode over to the window, his back to her. "There's more to being a father than a few minutes in the sack, Kelly."

"But I haven't asked you to be that kind of father."

"That's the only kind of father I will ever be. When I bring a child into this world, I won't abandon it!" He turned to glare at her.

Once more she regretted that the one man she thought would be the perfect father should have a conscience. But maybe that was what made him so perfect.

She must have had a niggling suspicion all along that he was different from the others on her list. That would explain why she'd avoided him until he was the only one left. She'd been afraid.

Now there was no one on her list.

With a sigh, she rose from the sofa. "Thank you at least for listening to me, James."

As she turned away, he pulled her around to face him, his hands on her shoulders. "Where are you going?"

"Home."

"That's it? You ask me to father your baby and then you walk away?" He seemed outraged at the idea.

"You told me no, James. What am I supposed to do? Try to seduce you?"

He jerked his hands away as if he feared she might try. "No. But—what are you going to do?"

"Go home."

"No, I mean about having a baby."

"I don't know." She could go to plan B, but it didn't appeal to her.

"Kelly, you can't go around asking men to father your baby." His voice was stern, like a father lecturing his child.

"That's my business, James."

"Have you asked anyone else?"

She turned away, anxious to leave. Also anxious to avoid the question.

"Well?"

"I considered some others."

"Did you ask them to father your child?"

"James, this is none of your business."

"The hell it isn't! You drop a bombshell on me like this and then plan on walking away?"

Kelly stared at him. He was getting angry all over again, and she didn't understand why. "What do you want from me?"

"An answer to my question would be a start."

"No. Okay? No, I didn't ask any of the others."

"Why?"

"Because I didn't want my baby to be like them."

"Oh, right. You chose me because I didn't wear braces," he said, not sounding very pleased about it.

"You didn't?" That was a question she'd forgotten to ask. When he glared at her even more, she said hurriedly, "James, I didn't mean to upset you. I just thought . . . you're a charming, intelligent man, a gentleman. And you have a sense of humor."

"Don't forget the lack of hereditary diseases. That's something in my favor, too."

His sarcasm was beginning to get on her nerves.

"Would you prefer that I didn't find you attractive? Shall I tell you that you repelled me? What do you want me to say, James?"

Perhaps he sensed the rising hysteria in her, because he clasped her shoulders again and his expression eased. "I'm sorry, Kelly. I didn't mean to go crazy on you. I—your question threw me off."

She stood there, saying nothing, staring into his dark blue eyes, wishing he'd given her a different answer.

"Look, I'm concerned about you. You can't go around asking just anyone to—to do this. You might get hurt."

"How?"

Her question appeared to stun him. Finally he said, "They might take you up on your offer."

She shook her head at him. "James, that's what I want. That's why I asked. I'm not stupid. I'm not going to ask someone if I don't think I'd enjoy—enjoy the process."

"The process? We're talking about making love, Kelly. That's a lot more personal than 'the process.'"

She closed her eyes and heaved a sigh. The man was demented. "I know that, James. Forget I ever asked, okay? It was a mistake."

"So you've abandoned the idea."

He made a statement, not a question, and Kelly didn't see the need to answer.

"Kelly?"

Taking her chin between his fingers, he nudged her face up so that she was reluctantly meeting his gaze. Okay, so he wasn't going to let her get away without answering. "I don't think I'll ask anyone else."

"So you won't have a baby."

She stared up at him, her lips pressed stubbornly together.

"Why aren't you agreeing with me?" he asked.

"Because it's still none of your business."

"I think it is."

"Well, you're wrong. It's my business, and it isn't something I've considered lightly. I've always wanted children, though I might not choose to have one this way. But if it will give my grandmother the will to live, then that's a good enough reason. She's the only family I have left."

"It will be kind of hard to accomplish if you don't ask for a man's help, won't it?" he asked, his gaze narrowed.

"Not really. A test tube will do just as well."

Maybe even better. Test tubes didn't demand answers. They didn't make you laugh. And they didn't have gorgeous blue eyes that would haunt a woman forever.

Chapter Three

The cradle rocked gently as he reached in to lift the small bundle, wrapped in a blue blanket, into his arms. Cuddling the warmth against him, he slowly peeled back the blanket. Kelly's green eyes stared up at him, and he blinked several times before he realized he was staring at a baby and not Kelly.

His baby.

That sense of ownership, of belonging, curled around his heart, enveloping it in a satisfying warmth. And surprise. When had he decided to have a child?

Kelly.

With that warmth still cuddled against him with one hand, he reached with the other for Kelly's stimulating curves. But she eluded him, a mysterious smile on her lips.

Suddenly everything changed. The child in his arms became a little boy, his hand trustingly enclosed in his. The little face smiling up at him looked amazingly like his own as a child, while he, as he saw himself, looked like his father. There, too, was the dog he'd had as a boy, jumping up to lick the child's face.

He ran across the meadow with the child, just catching a glimpse of an auburn-haired beauty who topped the hill just ahead of them.

Kelly.

"Mama," the child beside him called.

He, too, tried to call to her, but it was as if he were muffled.

Everything blurred, as if he were racing past inanimate objects before thudding to a halt. He found himself at a ball game, the boy still beside him, cheering as the bat cracked against the ball.

"This is great, Daddy," the child exclaimed, his beaming smile intensifying the warmth of his happiness. Turning to his other side, James found the elusive Kelly beside them. Both he and the child reached out for her, but she faded away.

James stirred. Sunlight filled his eyes as he opened them. When he realized the images he'd just seen were dreams, an inexplicable sadness filled him.

Ridiculous!

He'd never been tempted by an eight-pound bundle totally dependent on others. One that required bottles, diapers, burping and probably other disgusting activities he didn't want to think about.

Of course, the earlier images of a little boy held an attraction he hadn't even realized he wanted. But if he had a son, he could teach him things, play ball with him, take him on camping trips.

James shook himself from such a serious mental lapse. What was wrong with him? He had no time for children. He had a business to run.

For what purpose?

That question stopped him as he was tying his tie, staring into the mirror over his bathroom sink. Where had it come from? His business was important. To him, at least. And to his customers. He gave good value for their money. And he would be missed if he suddenly packed it in.

Which is what he'd have to do when he reached a certain age. There wouldn't be anyone to carry on.

He was being absurd. He had carried on his father's business, expanding it, increasing both the customer base and the volume. But his father had never forced him to do so.

Memory of his father's pride when he'd joined the family firm came back to him. Dad had been quick to introduce him to everyone with the words, *my son.* When his father had decided to retire, to enjoy the fruits of his labor, he'd told James he could do so because he knew he was leaving the company, his "other" child, in good hands.

But that wasn't a reason to have a child.

He had certainly never considered it as one.

And he didn't now.

"Mr. Townsend?"

"Hmm?" James turned away from the window,

bringing his thoughts back to the business at hand. His concentration hadn't improved since he first awoke.

"We need a decision right away, Mr. Townsend," his assistant, Peter Worth, said.

He studied the younger man. "Peter, do you and your wife plan to have a family?"

The abrupt question flustered the man. He'd received his promotion only a month ago and was still on tenterhooks, afraid of making a mistake. "What?" He met James's gaze and stammered, "I—I beg your pardon? I mean—"

"Relax, Peter. This isn't a test. And I have no business asking the question. I just wondered if you and your wife intended to have a family."

"Yes, sir, we do. We just—just wanted to wait until we were settled."

"Children are a big responsibility."

"Yes, sir." Peter's eyes were wide, as if he thought his boss had gone off his rocker.

James smiled. "No, I'm not crazy, Peter. And by the way, I think it's time you called me James."

Peter gulped. "Yes, sir."

James sighed and dealt with the question Peter needed answered. After the young man had left the office, James turned back to the phone and quickly dialed a number.

"Cecilia? This is James."

His cousin had lived all her life in Highland Park, the wealthy enclave near downtown Dallas where Kelly lived, and the two women were about the same age—twenty-eight or -nine, he thought.

"Hi, James. What's up?"

"Nothing much. I just hadn't talked to you in a few days."

After a moment of dead silence, Cecilia broke into a chuckle. "Yeah, sure. Now, what do you need?"

"Ceci, my feelings are hurt," James teased. She was his favorite relative.

"If you had any. You're cold, James, and you know it. Susan will never recover." The past month, in spite of his warnings, his cousin had tried her hand at matchmaking—with disastrous results.

"I didn't try to hurt her feelings, Ceci. But Susan wants to get married. You know that's not what I have in mind."

"How long are you going to let that bitch Denise ruin your life?"

"Shame on you, Cecilia, using such terrible language." James didn't want another postmortem of his marriage. "Ceci, can I ask you something?" he said before she could continue the subject.

There must have been something in his voice that alerted her, because she grew serious. "Sure, James."

"Did you and Rob— Was having children a conscious decision?"

"Yes. We discussed it before we married. Why?"

"I just wondered. I was discussing children with someone last night."

"You're thinking of having one? Aunt Carolyn would be thrilled," she said, referring to his mother. "But don't you need a wife first?"

"Don't be ridiculous. *I'm* not thinking of having any. My friend was talking about it. I just wondered if you ever regretted, you know, tying yourself down."

"I seriously regretted it at every 4:00 a.m. feeding, James, but that's all. The kids are…such a special part of our lives. I don't know that I can explain it, other than to say that they make our lives complete."

He mulled over the emotion he heard in Ceci's voice. It was a lot more than self-gratification or something temporary. He was pretty sure it was love. There was a flash of remembrance to his early-morning dream.

"Is that why you called?" Ceci asked quietly.

Drawn from his thoughts, afraid he'd revealed too much about his own state of mind, James tried to shrug off her question. "Yeah, I guess so. Oh, by the way, the other day I met someone I think you know."

"Who?"

"Kelly Abbott."

"Kelly? How is she? I haven't seen her in ages."

"She still lives here in Dallas."

"I know. But the last I heard she's still single, so our lives go in different— What do you mean, you met her? Are you two dating?"

"We had dinner together one night. I'm using the ad agency she works for, that's all."

"Uh-huh. Is she still as gorgeous as ever?"

James smiled. Leave it to Ceci to go straight for the jugular. "I'm afraid so."

"Well, be nice to her. She's special."

"Yeah. Do you know much about what's been going on with her the last few years?"

"Nope. I could ask around."

"Not on my part. I was just curious. I probably won't even see her again," he hurriedly added, knowing how quickly Ceci zeroed in on something.

"But, James—"

"I've got to go, Ceci. I'll talk to you in a few days."

He hung up the receiver before she could protest, or ask any questions he didn't want to answer.

AS ONE OF THE TOP advertising firms in the city, Bauer, Tate & Warner had more business than it could handle. Usually, Kelly lost herself in the demands of her work. Today, she caught herself staring into space.

She was about to make a momentous change in her life. Her decision still made sense to her, but the reality of it hadn't hit her until she had awakened that morning from a vivid dream, so real she'd almost cried at its disappearance.

She'd held her baby in her arms, a small package of energy and warmth. When she pulled back the blanket, the baby smiled at her. She turned to share her happiness with the father beside her—but the man had no face.

Even more frightening than the faceless form was the disappointment that filled her when she realized he wasn't James. She awoke screaming.

Not James Townsend. He wasn't interested. Kelly faced her disappointment. She'd always known she might have to go the artificial insemination route. Somehow, it just seemed colder, more impersonal, after last night. A faceless, nameless person as the father of her baby was distressing after picturing James in that role.

But she was going ahead with her plan. She'd always wanted children. In fact, when she'd been engaged, just after college, she'd planned on having a houseful of kids. She didn't want any child of hers to be an only one, as she had been.

Those plans disappeared with her engagement, when she found her fiancé in bed with one of her friends. She'd retreated from men for several years. Then, with time, she'd had several relationships, but none had turned into anything permanent.

She was approaching thirty, and she wanted a child. Still, she wouldn't go ahead, she thought, if it weren't for Gran. But something had to shock her grandmother from her lethargy. And if a side benefit of Gran getting well was a child, Kelly would welcome a baby with all her heart. Her fingers unconsciously moved, sketching, as she frequently did, her thoughts.

"Mornin', Kelly," a deep voice boomed. Tex Warner was the driving force behind the agency. A big man, he never entered a room without everyone knowing it.

"How's the Baker account coming along?" he asked as he put his hand on her shoulder and looked at her drawing board. "Babies?"

For the first time, Kelly really looked at her sketches. Her cheeks burned and she hastily ripped the sheet from her pad.

"Sorry, Tex. I'm not quite on track yet this morning."

"No problem, Kelly. I know you'll come up with somethin' spectacular." The big man leaned an arm on her table. "By the way, you know James Townsend?"

The piece of charcoal snapped in her fingers. "I've met him," she said cautiously.

"So he said. He was impressed," Tex said, wandering around her small office, picking up different items and then replacing them.

"He—he was?"

"Yeah. Good thing, too. Townsend's one of our biggest accounts. Want to keep him happy." He turned to stare at Kelly. "Not that I'm suggesting you do anything improper, mind you." He sighed. "Lordy, even the hint of such a thing, and your grandma would be all over me." His big body shivered with mock fear of a ninety-eight-pound elderly woman.

Kelly grinned, as he'd intended, then shrugged her shoulders. "I'm not working on Mr. Townsend's account."

"Not right now. But he was mighty curious about your work."

James Townsend had expressed almost no interest in her work last evening. What was the man up to? Why would he have called Tex? Surely he didn't reveal anything about last night to Tex. Her eyes widened in apprehension, but before she could ask her employer anything, Linda Vinson, one of her co-workers, stuck her head in the door.

"Kelly? Did you forget— Oh! Good morning, Tex," Linda said, acknowledging her boss's presence. "I was just going to remind Kelly of our meeting."

"The Baker project? Good, good. We need to get that wrapped up. There are a lot of projects waiting on the assembly line." He shot a significant look at Kelly. "Well, on your way, Kelly. I don't pay you to sit around doin' nothing," he said with his booming laugh. Since he usually urged her not to work so hard, she didn't worry about his teasing.

She'd hesitated about going to work for him after she finished college. He and his wife, Ann, were old family friends. But her grandparents had urged her to accept his offer. Tex himself had promised her no special privileges and a lot of hard work. He'd kept his word.

"I'll be right there, Linda." As soon as her friend had disappeared, she stepped to Tex's side and kissed his cheek. "I'll try not to let you down, Tex."

"I'm not losing any sleep worryin' about you, honey." He wiped the tenderness from his voice and returned to his normal high-voltage voice. "Now get to work."

Kelly grinned and gave him a mock salute before gathering her file on the Baker project and hurrying from her office.

After she'd left, Tex Warner pulled the discarded sheet from the trash can. "Babies, huh?"

JAMES WANDERED DOWN the aisle of the bookstore, surreptitiously looking for anyone he might know. Finally satisfied that he was surrounded by strangers, he searched the signs and found the one he was looking for.

Parenting.

His eyes widened at the number of titles. It seemed every doctor who ever existed had written a book on having a baby, parenting a baby, teaching a baby. There was even one on how to make good home movies of your baby.

"May I help you, sir?"

He turned to look at the young woman standing at his elbow, a cheerful look on her face. The name tag said she was Lisa.

"I'm just looking."

"All right. If I can help you, let me know."

She turned to go and he changed his mind. The longer he stood here, the more likely he'd see someone he knew. Better to get some help. "Can you recommend one of these books?"

Lisa spun around and looked at the shelf he was pointing at. "Baby books?"

He nodded, subduing the urge to ask her to lower her voice.

"Is your wife already preggers or just trying?"

Wondering if book store clerks enjoyed the same privilege as doctors when it came to a client's private life, he replied, "Just thinking about it."

"Oh, well, then you'll need one that covers everything. We sell a lot of this one." She pulled a thick book from the shelf, a pregnant woman pictured on the cover, her husband with his hand on her enlarged stomach. "It will tell you all you need to know."

"Okay, thanks." Without looking inside it, he headed immediately for the check-out counter, keeping the book pressed to his side.

"There's also one about home delivery," Lisa called out. He'd already gotten several aisles away. Never breaking his stride, he waved his thanks for that additional, if totally useless, information.

After taking his money, the cashier asked, "Would you care for a bag, sir?"

"Yes, I'd like a bag," he snapped, not anxious to share his purchase with anyone he encountered. When he saw the stricken look on her face, he immediately apologized. "I'm sorry. I'm running late and didn't— I'm sorry." He grabbed his package and left.

"WHY DON'T WE WATCH 'The Cosby Show' rerun tonight, Gran? You like that show, don't you?" Kelly asked, watching her grandmother closely.

Elizabeth Abbott barely nodded her head, but Kelly took that as a good sign.

"Try to eat a little more chicken. Mary did a good job baking it." Mary, the widow she'd hired to look after her grandmother recently, had been a godsend. She even stayed late when Kelly had to go out, which had happened a lot lately. Kelly got up and poured herself more ice tea.

"Did I tell you Tex asked about you today? He wanted to know how you were doing."

"That's nice," Elizabeth responded. She laid down her fork and took a small sip of ice tea.

Kelly continued chattering, searching for different subjects her grandmother might find interesting. The strain of these meals was growing worse every day.

As she'd told James, she'd taken her grandmother to several doctors. Finally, one of the most respected had said that her grandmother was dying of a broken heart.

Kelly had stared at him, incredulous.

"Miss Abbott, we can do amazing things these days in medicine, but we can't save a patient who doesn't want to be saved. Your grandmother is one of those people."

"But what can I do?"

"I don't know that you can do anything. There's nothing physically wrong with her. If you can find something that will interest her, snap her out of her despondency, I believe she could live another ten or fifteen years. If not, well, I don't think she'll last another three months."

That was when Kelly hatched The Plan.

"Try some more potatoes, Gran."

"I'm just not hungry, dear," she said with a small sigh that wrenched Kelly's heart.

"I remember when I first came to live with you and Granddad. I didn't want to eat, either," Kelly reminded her. Those first days after her mother's sudden death in a car accident had been difficult. "But you never let me get away with that excuse."

The faintest smile touched Gran's lips, filling Kelly with triumph. "You were a child, dear. I'm an adult. You shouldn't have to bother with me."

"You're never a bother, Gran."

"You have your own life to lead, child. You shouldn't be living here with an old woman." Elizabeth looked away, her face pale, her voice tired.

"You didn't need a child in your life when I came to live with you. But you took me in." Kelly swallowed the tears that filled her eyes. She always tried to be cheerful with her grandmother.

"But you weren't a bother. Henry and I—" Elizabeth paused and pressed her lips tightly together. She still couldn't talk about her husband easily, even though it had been four months since he died.

"Because we're family, right, Gran? That's what you always told me. And that's why you're not a burden to me."

Another little smile formed on Elizabeth's lips. "All right,. child. I won't argue with you anymore. And I have to say you're an awfully good girl."

Kelly smiled in relief. Those words had been a mantra of forgiveness when she'd broken any rules as a child. Gran hadn't ever wanted her to think her grandparents hadn't loved her. "Thanks, Gran. But I learned from you. You're the best awfully good girl I know."

The telephone interrupted them. She crossed the kitchen to pick up the receiver.

"Hello?"

"Kelly? This is James Townsend."

Her teeth sank into her bottom lip and she turned away from her grandmother. "Yes?"

"How are you?"

She looked back over her shoulder at her grandmother who had given up all pretense of eating and now sat staring into space. "I'm fine."

"I wondered if I could drop by."

"What? Now?"

"Yes. Are you busy?"

Busy? No, but she didn't want James Townsend coming here. "My grandmother isn't feeling well. I don't think—"

"I won't stay long. I just wanted to talk to you.

"Now isn't a good time."

"I could come later, if that's better." He was refusing to take no for an answer. "I have something for you."

He had something for her.

After Kelly hung up the phone, she stood there, thinking.

What could he have possibly meant? The only thing she wanted from him he'd refused to give her.

Chapter Four

"Who was on the phone, dear?" Elizabeth Abbott asked, watching her granddaughter more closely than she had in a long time. Normally, she wouldn't think of questioning Kelly about her calls, but the child was suddenly nervous, making Elizabeth think something was wrong.

Kelly was helping her to bed, just as she always did. Elizabeth had waited to ask her the question, unsure if she should. But if something was wrong, Henry would never forgive her if she didn't help their darling grandchild.

"A client, Gran. He—he's bringing over an idea he had about his ad campaign."

"At night? Surely Tex doesn't expect you to work all evening, too? I'll talk to him. Your evenings should be your own time, Kelly." She tried to make her voice sound firm, but even to her own ears it was soft, with no conviction. She frowned in irritation.

"No, Gran, that's not necessary. I'm talking to him because—because I'm interested. Tex has nothing to do with his coming over."

"Who is he?" Her voice might be weak, but her mind still worked. Something didn't sound right.

"James Townsend. He owns a plastics firm. They make the dishes the airlines use."

Her granddaughter clicked off the lamp beside the bed and then leaned down to kiss her cheek. "Get a good night's sleep, Gran. Call if you need anything."

"I will. Good night."

After Kelly closed her door, leaving her alone, Elizabeth thought about what Kelly had said. The words were right. But there was a tension in Kelly's voice that told her differently.

What should she do? For the first time in weeks the urge to act filled her. She could sneak downstairs and eavesdrop. But she hated to treat Kelly as a child. Even as she was debating the ethics of such action, her eyes drifted shut. Tomorrow, she promised herself. Tomorrow she would find out what was troubling Kelly.

NOW THAT HE WAS HERE, James wondered if he'd made a mistake. He punched the doorbell as if it was at fault, instead of him. In his other hand he held the book he'd bought earlier in the day.

When the door swung open, he forgot all his misgivings. Kelly stared at him, questions in her big green eyes, and he wished he had the right to pull her into his arms. She had her hair tied back in some kind of ponytail, but soft curls framed her face.

Without saying anything, she stood back and gestured for him to enter. He moved past her, feeling the heat of her body as he did so.

"Please have a seat. I hope you didn't mind waiting until later to come. I thought it best if Gran didn't know, and she's gone to bed now."

"We're only talking, Kelly. There's nothing to hide from your grandmother, but I didn't mind waiting."

She looked on edge and didn't respond directly to his comment, only saying hurriedly, "I'll go get us some ice tea."

James studied the room while she was gone. It was furnished with antiques and several beautiful flower arrangements. He liked it. It somehow seemed warmer than his professionally decorated apartment, as if a family lived there.

The sound of approaching footsteps drew his thoughts back to his hostess. He lay the book on the carpet beside the sofa, his mind more on Kelly than his gift. His reaction to her alarmed him. He'd thought his visit was somewhat of a whim, but his first glance confirmed what he should've known all along. He'd wanted to see her. Needed to see her.

She entered the room with two glasses and handed him one before sitting down on a brocaded Victorian couch. He joined her there, surprised to find how comfortable it was.

"You said you needed to see me?"

"Yes. I wanted to apologize for—for my behavior last night. I think I got a little pushy toward the end. I had no right to demand that you tell me anything."

Even though he was apologizing, he wasn't sure he understood his reaction. They had been discussing the possibility of sharing an incredibly intimate event, and then she'd turned and walked away. He'd felt—rejected, alone, confused.

"Thank you for apologizing. I didn't understand why you reacted as you did." Her eyes wide, she stared at him as her teeth sank into her bottom lip.

Forcing back a groan, he swallowed and looked away. "I'm not sure I can explain. Our conversation was...disturbing."

"I'm sorry."

"Have you given it any more thought?" He was doing it again, asking questions he had no right to ask, but he couldn't help himself.

"You mean having a baby?"

He nodded, his gaze traveling over her delicate features. Would her baby have red hair? Or would it favor its father?

She looked away. "I haven't stopped thinking about it since I first came up with the idea. I haven't changed my mind, if that's what you're asking."

"May I ask you another question?"

"Yes."

"Why won't you consider marriage?" He wasn't sure she would answer, but he wanted to know.

After taking a sip of her tea, she set it down on the coffee table and laced her fingers together, staring down at them. Finally, she raised her head and looked at him. "It's important that Gran think I'm alone, abandoned. Otherwise, she'd just assume my husband would take care of me." She shrugged and then added, "I'm afraid I'm a little cynical, too, James. I haven't had much luck in the men department, and I don't expect to."

"So you don't believe in marriage?"

"Do you?"

"For some people. My parents have been happy for thirty-eight years."

"Gran and Granddad were married for over fifty years," she said, her features softening. "They meant everything to each other."

There was a hunger in her eyes that tugged at his heart. He reached out and covered her clasped hands with one of his. "Don't you think you should give the idea of marriage another try? You could have the same kind of marriage as your grandparents."

She jerked her hands away from his and rose. Moving across the room, she turned to face him, her arms crossed in front of her. "Do you often give advice you're not willing to take yourself?"

Though her aim was true, he tried to hide any reaction behind a grim smile. "Just because marriage didn't work for me doesn't mean it won't work for someone else."

"So your divorce exempts you from the 'try it, you'll like it' group?"

"Maybe. At least I've tried it."

"Does being engaged qualify me? Because I certainly came close to marriage, and I think that experience ought to count for something." She turned her back on him and crossed the room to stare out the window.

He frowned. Rising from the sofa, he moved over to stand behind her. "What happened?"

She whirled around to face him, her hands on her hips, a stubborn look on her face that James thought made her look very kissable.

"Isn't this where you came in? Apologizing for questions you had no business asking?"

He slanted an acknowledging grin at her. "Nosy, aren't I?" If her reaction was any measure of his charm, it was nonexistent. He tried again. "I know I have no business asking, but I'm concerned about you. I don't think electing to be a single parent is wise."

"Thank you for your concern, James, but this is my decision. Once you refused my request, you had nothing to do with it."

Though her voice was firm, her stance aggressive, James clasped her shoulders and felt her trembling. Why couldn't he accept her refusal and walk away? Why did he have to keep touching her?

"Kelly, I want to be friends. I may not be able to— to do what you asked, but I'd like to be there for you. You'll need a friend if you go ahead with your plan."

She drew in a deep breath that he felt with every inch of his body as he watched her breasts push against the sweatshirt she wore. "No. I need Gran to think I'm all alone, that I need *her* and no one else."

They stood frozen, staring into each other's eyes. James didn't realize he was leaning toward her until she broke away and turned, rubbing her palms on her jean-clad thighs.

"Have you really thought about the change this— this baby would make in your life?"

She spun back around, exasperation on her face. "Really, James! Do you think I'm an idiot?"

"No, I didn't mean to offend you, but it *is* a big change."

"I know." With a rueful chuckle, she added, "I can remember some of the things I put Gran and Grand-dad through. They hadn't planned on raising their grandchild."

He moved closer, drawn by the sweetness of her smile. "Were you a problem child?"

She shook her head. "Not really. I was confused, frightened. They were always there for me, showing me the way, loving me."

"Yeah," he said, clearing his suddenly thick throat. "My parents were pretty patient with me, too. Dad tried to teach me to pitch. After I broke the same window three times, he suggested tennis."

"Don't you—" She broke off and turned away.

"What, Kelly?" he asked, following her.

"It's a silly question, but don't you feel an obligation to pass that love on?" She shook her head in frustration. "Maybe *obligation* is the wrong word. Even if it weren't for Gran, I'd want to have a child. To share with, to teach, to—to see the world again through fresh eyes." She looked at him, her passion visible on her face.

His objections to her plans drowned in the depth of her gaze. "You'll make a great mother, Kelly."

"I hope so. I want my baby to have a happy childhood, to love life."

She wrapped her arms around her waist, as if she already carried a child within her. James was reminded of the picture on the cover of the book he purchased.

"Remember I said I had something for you?" he asked abruptly. He walked back to the sofa where he'd left the book. "I was in a bookstore today and I found this. The salesclerk said it was popular. I thought you might find it useful."

She stared at him in surprise. "You bought a book for me?"

He held out the book but stepped back as her fingers touched his. Clearing his throat, he explained, "I was a Boy Scout. I believe in being prepared."

"I can see you in a little uniform," she teased, a sudden grin on her face. "I think if I have a boy I'll get him involved in stuff like that."

"I'll volunteer to teach him tennis. And we could try baseball if you're not too fond of your windows," he teased, taking a step closer. He couldn't resist her smile.

The warmth fled her face and she looked uncomfortable. "That's very nice of you, James, but I'm sure you'll have your own life to lead. After all, we're talking six or seven years down the road. We—we may not even know each other then."

He wanted to protest her words. They felt wrong, hurtful, but they could be true. "I don't think I'll ever forget you, Kelly."

How could he? Her green eyes sparkled like emeralds when she was happy. If her eyes filled with tears, they reminded him of a forest in a rainstorm. And her smile. No, he couldn't forget her.

"I guess not. Not too many women make a request like mine."

"At least not on the first date," he agreed, a smile returning to his face. He stepped closer to her, his hands reaching for her shoulders again. "Have you gone to the sperm bank yet?"

"No. I couldn't today. I had several meetings to attend."

He fought the compelling urge to change his answer to her all-important question. He couldn't agree to father a baby and then abandon it, walk away. Besides, he didn't have room for a child in his life. What was he thinking of?

Maybe he wasn't thinking at all. Maybe he was responding to Kelly's closeness, wishing he could pull her into his arms, feel her move against him.

He jerked his hands away. "I'd better go. I just wanted to bring the book by."

"It was very thoughtful of you, James."

"Yeah." He strode to the door but found he couldn't leave quite yet. She'd occupied his mind for the past twenty-four hours. As much as her request had startled him, the intense attraction had not. He'd known she would tempt him to touch, to hold. And she did.

She followed him, and he gave in to the impulse that had haunted him for twenty-four hours. Swiftly he bent and caressed her lips with his.

She barely gasped, the air fluttering against his lips, before she accepted his touch, her mouth warming, softening to his.

He pulled away and stared at her, stunned by the desire that surged through him. The urge to pull her against him, wrap his arms around her, deepen the kiss until he tasted her very soul, flooded him. But he didn't dare give in to that urge.

She stood quietly waiting, as if she expected something from him.

"I— Good luck, Kelly."

Without waiting for her to speak, he hurried to his car, afraid if he didn't, he might never remember his objections to Kelly's plan. He needed to put some distance between him and the powerful attraction he felt for her.

But he could still taste her on his lips.

KELLY STRUGGLED to cover up the dark circles under her eyes the next morning. Sleep had been almost impossible after her conversation with James.

His visit hadn't changed her mind. But it had disappointed her. How she would have liked her child to be like James. He was a good man. Why hadn't she met him before she'd made her plans?

With a sigh, she reminded herself that thoughts of James Townsend had to be set aside. It was just as well. Staying unemotional about the man might be more of a challenge than she could face.

She trudged up the stairs with her grandmother's breakfast tray and entered the room without her customary bright smile. Greeting Gran, she positioned her against the pillows and set the tray in place.

"I'll see you this evening, Gran," she said as she kissed her cheek.

"Kelly? Is anything wrong?"

Wearily, Kelly looked at the small lady lying against the pillows. "Wrong? No, nothing's wrong."

"You look a little tired. Are you trying to do too much?"

"No, Gran, everything's fine. Don't you worry about anything."

"Did you and Mr. Townsend have a good meeting?"

Kelly stared at her grandmother, wondering if she'd overheard any of their discussion. "Yes. Yes, we had a most . . . most productive meeting, Gran."

"What's he like?"

Kelly stared into space, picturing James Townsend, his dark good looks, blue eyes, athletic form. Any child of his would be beautiful.

"Kelly?"

"What, Gran?" She couldn't remember if her grandmother had asked her a question or not.

"How old is Mr. Townsend?"

Blinking several times in surprise, Kelly finally said, "I think he's about thirty-four or -five, Gran. I'm not sure. Tex doesn't care how old they are as long as they can pay the bill."

"Seems awfully young to own his own company."

"It was his father's originally. But he's taken it over and expanded it quite a bit."

"Ah. His wife must be very proud of him."

Kelly frowned. "He's not married, Gran—at least not now. I've got to run or I'll be late." She gave her grandmother a kiss. "You take care of yourself, okay? Mary will be here soon."

"I will, Kelly, dear."

Elizabeth Abbott stared at the door long after it had closed behind Kelly. Her granddaughter's responses to her questions had been very interesting.

Elizabeth wished she'd stayed up last night to meet this James Townsend. Was he trying to get a move on—no, that wasn't right. What did they say these days? Make a move, that was it. Was he trying to make a move on Kelly?

She and Henry had done their best to love and care for Kelly. Just because Henry was gone didn't mean she could let someone hurt her child.

She needed to find out more about James Townsend.

Chapter Five

James unconsciously massaged his temples.

"A headache, Mr. Townsend?" Peter Worth asked.

Without raising his gaze, James said, "I thought I asked you to call me James. And yes, I have a headache. See if you can find me some aspirin."

"Yes, sir—that is, James. I'll be right back."

He would, too. Peter had been hovering all morning. James had had no idea he could inspire his assistant to be such a mother hen. After a week out of town, traveling on business, he didn't mind a little assistance. But he didn't think Peter could help him with what was really stealing his rest.

He couldn't stop thinking about Kelly and the child she wanted. After their conversation last week, he knew she'd be a wonderful mother. But he still believed a child should have two parents. Raising a child was a gamble at best. Why handicap yourself?

If being a single parent was so easy, he'd consider it himself.

Whoa! Where had that idea come from?

He leaned back in his swivel chair, alarmed by the trend of his thoughts. Okay, so his talk with Kelly had his mind on a different track than it normally pursued. And the dream that had haunted him the past week had him thinking differently. Lonely hotel rooms left him with a lot of time to consider the future.

When he'd first married, he'd assumed he and Denise would have children in the future, the distant future. Then he'd discovered there were no guarantees in marriage. After their divorce, he'd been bitter, cynical. That's when his father decided to retire.

As the idea struck him, James immediately rejected it. His father wouldn't have retired just to help him get over his divorce. That was ridiculous. Wasn't it?

He couldn't be sure. He knew that the plan, if it was that, had worked. He'd buried himself in the growth and expansion of the company. Women had played a peripheral role in his life, providing occasional entertainment and little else.

Until Kelly.

Not that he would consider remarrying, even if that was what she had in mind. He'd decided he was better cut out to be single. But his conversations with her had awakened an awareness, a look toward the future that disturbed him.

Picking up the phone, he pushed the fast-dial button that would connect him to his parents in Arizona.

"Mom, how are you?"

"James? Richard, it's James," his mother called and James heard the extension being picked up.

He greeted his father and they exchanged the usual questions about his father's golf game, his mother's bridge tournament and the weather. Finally he got to the purpose of his call.

"Mom, Dad, why did you decide to retire when you did?"

Startled silence greeted his question. Finally his mother asked cautiously, "What do you mean?"

"It suddenly occurred to me today that the timing was fortuitous for me, coming as it did when I was feeling so low after the divorce." Neither parent said anything. "Did my divorce have anything to do with your decision?"

Richard Townsend cleared his throat. "Well, son, uh, you know I'd been wanting to improve my golf game. And besides, competition is better left to the young. Look what you've done for the company. It proves my decision was the right one."

"In other words," James said, "the answer is yes."

"Not an unqualified yes. Your mother and I talked it over. We were both kind of tired of the rat race. Once we got down here, we knew we'd made the right decision. Our only regret was leaving you up there alone."

James's sister, Melinda, along with her husband and two children, lived in Phoenix, close to his parents.

"James, why are you asking now? What's happened?" his mother asked, an anxious note in her voice.

"Everything's fine, Mom," he reassured her. "I was just talking to someone last week, and it's made me look at things a little differently."

"A female someone?"

The hopeful note in her voice made him shake his head ruefully. She never gave up.

"Mom, I'm not going to marry again. Remember?"

"Then how am I going to get more grandchildren? Melissa and Bryan are six and eight. They won't even let me hold them anymore."

"Now, Carolyn, don't hound the boy. He has to do what he thinks is best."

"But, Richard, I don't want him to be alone!"

"Mom, I'm fine. Look, I have to go, but I just want to thank you for what you did. I—I hope you're happy with the decision. It was a big sacrifice to make. I don't know how to repay you."

"You don't repay us, son," Richard said, his voice deep with feeling. "We love you. If you get the chance, you help out someone else, that's all."

"Preferably, your own child," Carolyn snuck in.

"Carolyn!" Richard protested.

Long after James said goodbye, he still couldn't put aside his thoughts.

He'd been so buried in his own misery at the time, he'd never stopped to think about his parents' decision. It stunned him that they had given up their home, their comfortable life, to help him. Not that they had

had to move to Siberia. They were well settled in Phoenix. But they had made the change for him.

He remembered Kelly's words. She'd chosen the word *obligation* and then changed her mind. Obligation would never be enough of a reason to have a child. But coupled with the love she had to give, and the love she had for her grandmother, it made her decision even more understandable.

It also made him reexamine his own decision. A child would make a huge difference in his life, for himself and his family. A happy difference. If he could have a child, without marriage, why not? Kelly had offered him an incredible opportunity, and he had turned it down.

Maybe it was time to reconsider his decision.

Without conscious thought, he reached for the phone and dialed Bauer, Tate & Warner.

"Kelly Abbott, please."

IT WAS ONE of those days when nothing seemed to go right. Kelly wadded up another sketch and aimed for the trash can. Not that she'd hit it. The littered floor testified to that.

On good days she never missed.

The phone rang and she swallowed her irritation. "Yes?"

"Kelly? It's James."

No need to ask James who. As much as she tried to put him from her mind, he'd dominated her thoughts for the past week. "Hi, James."

"I wondered if I could take you to lunch."

His husky voice sent shivers down her, and she stiffened her spine. Time to rid herself of temptation. "Thank you, anyway, James, but it's kind of a hectic day."

"I really do need to talk to you about—about what we've discussed, Kelly. When can we meet? Tonight? Tomorrow?"

Part of James's charm was his determination—until it was directed at her.

"Maybe I can work in a quick lunch. Where shall I meet you?"

He named an expensive, quiet restaurant, well-known in Dallas. "Would twelve noon be okay?"

"Look, why don't we go somewhere simple, fast? The Cactus Grill or—"

"Because everyone would overhear our conversation. Do you want that?"

His words stopped her cold. No, she didn't want that. With a sigh, she succumbed to his suggestion. "Okay."

"I could pick you up, so we'd only have one car there," he added.

"No. I'll meet you at the restaurant."

She'd need her car to keep from being alone with him—and in case she had to make a fast escape. Around James she was tempted to do something foolish, because the biggest danger James Townsend represented was the attraction she felt for him.

Since she hadn't heard from him for a week, not since he came to her house, she'd assumed he'd wiped her request from his mind. She was left to regret meeting him.

Why now? If she weren't about to embark on her campaign to save Gran, she might have wanted to pursue something with James. She knew he wasn't interested in marriage, but... She shook her head. Foolish thoughts. Better to keep her focus on the immediate future. She had enough problems there.

Almost two hours later, she was escorted by a solicitous maître d' to James's table.

"Kelly, I'm glad you could make it," James said as he stood to greet her with a smile that could light up a woman's heart.

"Tex would never forgive me if I disappointed one of his favorite clients," she returned, determined to distance herself from him.

"This isn't business and you know it." His smile had disappeared.

She gave a little shrug and picked up the menu. When she dared to look up, he was still frowning at her, his stare intent.

Before he could say anything, the waiter appeared at their table to take their drink orders and tell them the specials of the day.

Kelly asked for a Diet Coke and continued to study the menu, avoiding James's gaze.

"Is that caffeine-free?" James asked. When the waiter shook his head no, James turned to her. "Kelly, maybe you should order some mineral water or something."

She stared at him, confused. What was the problem? "You object to my ordering Diet Coke?"

"It has caffeine."

He wasn't making any sense. "I know."

"Didn't you read the book I gave you?"

Realization flooded her. She looked up at the waiter, his gaze impatient, and repeated firmly, "I'll have Diet Coke, please."

"Yes, madam. And you, sir?"

James asked for ice tea and waited for the man to leave. As soon as they were alone again, he said, "Kelly—"

"No! James, I am not yet—"

"I know that! But the book says you should clear the caffeine from your system. It's not good for the baby."

"Shh!" She closed her eyes. Maybe when she opened them she would find herself alone . . . and safe from temptation.

"You need to read the book, Kelly. You don't look like you're getting enough rest, either. Eight hours is recommended."

"Thank you, Doctor," she muttered. "Anything else?"

"Exercise?"

"I wasn't serious, James. You are not a medical doctor. And whatever happens in the near future, you will not be involved. Remember?"

Whatever he would have said in response was lost because a distinguished-looking man stopped at their table. "James! I haven't seen you in ages." The man nodded at Kelly, curiosity in his eyes. "How's your father?"

"Fine, George," James replied, standing and offering his hand. "Kelly, this is George Canfield, an old friend. Kelly Abbott."

Mr. Canfield took Kelly's extended hand. "How do you do, Kelly? James, your lunch companions have improved considerably."

The implication was obvious and Kelly rushed to correct it. "I'm with Bauer, Tate & Warner, Mr. Canfield, James's advertising agency."

"Oh. A business luncheon? Too bad for James, but good for me. May I join you? I've been thinking about doing a little advertising myself. Your firm is supposed to be one of the best."

"We are. I'd be delighted for you to join us...if you don't mind, James?" She knew the true answer to her question, but fortunately, James didn't give it.

"Of course I don't mind. Sit down, George."

With a hidden sigh of relief, Kelly turned her thoughts to business, a much safer topic than whatever James wanted to discuss.

BY THE TIME lunch was finished, James had a greater appreciation for Kelly's business talents. And a greater frustration, too.

She had incredible communications skills, considerable advertising acumen, marketing knowledge, and a charm that never descended to flirtatiousness. George Canfield had been reeled in—hook, line and sinker.

And James had twiddled his thumbs.

All three rose and Kelly and George shook hands. When she extended her hand to him, James stared at it, as if he didn't understand what she was doing.

"James, the lady is offerin' to shake your hand," George pointed out. "I think maybe you went to sleep while we were doin' business. Hope you didn't mind."

James took Kelly's hand, holding it a minute too long, glaring at her fiercely. After all that had passed between them, she wanted to shake his hand, like a stranger? She'd asked him to father her child, damn it!

She flashed her gaze to George and back again, and he reluctantly turned to the older man. "I guess my mind was on other things, George, but no, I didn't mind. You've made a wise choice."

"I think so, too. You tell your daddy I said hi, and I'll see you in a couple of days, little lady." With a beaming smile, he walked away.

"You don't object to being called little lady?" James muttered under his breath as he took her arm.

"Mr. Canfield is about the same age as Gran. I didn't find his manner offensive in the least." She pulled her arm away and rushed from the restaurant.

"What's the hurry?" he asked as he caught up with her on the sidewalk outside. It was mid-September, but in Texas that meant the summer heat wave still had its grip on the city.

"I have to get back to the office. I didn't intend to stay away so long."

"Now, wait just a minute," he protested, taking her arm again. "You picked up a new client. Tex will forgive you if you're a little late from lunch. We haven't had a chance to talk."

"I don't think we have anything to talk about," she offered and moved aside as a group of businessmen exited the restaurant.

Grimly he looked around him. "We can't talk here with the world passing by. Take a walk with me in the park over there."

"James, it's hot! And besides—"

"Kelly, we are going to talk. It can be in the park, or I can camp on your doorstep all night. Which is it going to be?"

The determined glint in his eyes must have convinced her because she sighed and nodded. "The park, then."

They crossed the street to the relative coolness of the shade provided by the trees.

MARY AND ELIZABETH were sitting in the den, watching one of the soap operas that dominated daytime television.

"That man is a bad one. He pretends to be interested in business, but all he does is go from one bed to another, leading those poor girls on," Mary complained, looking up from her knitting.

Elizabeth didn't answer her, but Mary wasn't surprised. She'd been taking care of the lady for three months now and Elizabeth seemed to take little interest in anything.

As if to prove her thoughts wrong, Elizabeth frowned at the television. "Men are sometimes wicked, aren't they?"

"That they are. Not my Billy, of course, or your Henry. They were of a different generation. But my neighbor's daughter—"

"Bring me the phone, Mary," Elizabeth said, an urgent note in her voice Mary hadn't heard before.

"Is anything the matter?"

"No, dear. I'm sorry I interrupted you. But I'm afraid Kelly has met a scalawag just like that man on television. I need to ask some questions."

Mary listened as Elizabeth dialed a number and asked to speak with Tex Warner. The one-sided conversation didn't tell her much. As soon as Elizabeth hung up the phone, Mary asked, "Well?"

"I don't know. Tex seems to like the man, but he didn't know Mr. Townsend came over last night to work on his advertising campaign."

"That doesn't sound very businesslike."

"And Kelly was nervous, tense. I should have stayed up and met the man. You can tell a lot about a man when you see him in person."

"That you can."

"Hmm. Mary, you and I are going to have to keep our ears open. I'm not having some man take advantage of my granddaughter."

Mary enjoyed Elizabeth's company, but she knew where her duty lay. "Now, Elizabeth, you know Kelly worries herself sick over you. She wouldn't want you to be upset."

"Mary, if it was your granddaughter, what would you do?"

Elizabeth was watching her with a smile.

"I think you know me too well, Elizabeth Abbott. You know if I'd been blessed with any children or grandchildren, I'd have done whatever I could to help them."

"Exactly. I'm making you an honorary aunt. Together we're going to protect my granddaughter! And not a word to Kelly. If she asks how I'm doing, you say 'just the same.' I don't want her upset even more."

Mary couldn't refuse to help. Elizabeth was right to protect Kelly. Besides, for the first time in months, the woman's cheeks were flushed and her eyes sparkling. As long as Mary didn't let her overdo, things might work out all right. And Kelly wouldn't even know what Elizabeth was up to.

Chapter Six

James led Kelly to a park bench positioned perfectly beneath a shade tree. She sat down, but he didn't join her. Anxiously she watched him as he began to pace. Somehow she was afraid she wouldn't like what he had to say.

"I've been having second thoughts. I think maybe you're right."

She blinked several times in surprise. "About what?" she asked cautiously. This wasn't what she expected.

"About having a baby."

Several responses crossed her mind, but she selected the most urgent. "Does this mean you're willing to help me?"

"Yes." He'd stopped pacing and stood facing her, a smile on his face.

"Just—just like that?"

"No, not just like that. I've hardly thought of anything else for the past week, but I've decided that a baby would be good for both of us."

The mixed emotions that filled her abruptly intensified. "What do you mean—'both of us'?"

He moved to the bench and sat beside her, taking her hand in his. "You need a baby for your grandmother. My parents want more grandchildren. And we both want a child." He held up his hand before she could speak. "I hadn't thought much about the future until you brought up the idea, but I want a son to carry on, to teach things to, like baseball, fishing—life. I want to be a father."

"James—" she began, needing to point out the one element of her plan that he'd forgotten, that would make his decision impossible, when she was interrupted.

"James!" A lone jogger, a tall blond woman in biker shorts, T-shirt and running shoes, abruptly halted her exercise to beam at Kelly's companion.

"Dana, hello," James responded, giving a light embrace as the woman extended her arms.

"What are you doing out here? I thought you never stopped working," she teased, but her gaze moved to Kelly and back to James.

"Just taking a break. I see you're staying fit as always," he said, smiling at her.

Kelly ground her teeth. Fit? The woman was an amazon, a well-proportioned amazon, and her workout clothes hid nothing. Kelly unconsciously sucked in her stomach as she watched Dana and James chat, then forced herself to relax. She wasn't competing with the other woman for James's attention.

"Well, I'd better go if I'm going to finish my exercising before my meeting at two o'clock. Give me a call sometimes, James," Dana said, sending him a longing look that irritated Kelly in spite of herself.

"I'll do that," James assured her, his hands in his pockets. Dana leaned forward to kiss his cheek and then jogged off.

"Sorry for the interruption, Kelly," he said, turning back to her.

"It appears you know everyone in Dallas," she grumbled.

"Not quite. You were saying?"

She didn't want to say what she'd been about to say. But she had to. And it was for the best. She couldn't remain uninvolved with James. She knew that now. And she would be too tempted, if she didn't have a good reason.

She drew a deep breath and said abruptly, "James, it won't work."

"What won't work?"

"Your being the father of my baby." She felt relief at finally having said what must be said. But there was an incredible sadness filling her also.

He scowled at her. "Why not? I'm perfectly healthy. I think we'd make a beautiful baby."

She hurriedly looked around. With their luck, half the people they knew would be listening. And she couldn't argue with what he'd said. She thought they'd make a beautiful baby, too.

"It's not that. You've forgotten something important."

"What have I forgotten?"

"I need to be alone, to convince Gran that I need her."

"That's ridiculous. I mean, I'm not offering marriage, Kelly. I only want to be a father to the baby."

Kelly shook her head. The whole point was to make Gran feel indispensable. And then there was the matter of protecting her heart.

"No, James."

James seized her shoulders, raising her to her feet. "Kelly, surely we can work this out. We both want the same thing. Why can't we work together?"

"Because Gran is important to me, James. Not just the child. You can find another woman to give you a child. I can't find another grandmother." She pulled from his grasp. "I have to go."

"We need to talk about this, Kelly," James insisted as she turned away.

"No, James, I don't think so. In fact, I think it would be better if we didn't talk anymore."

She walked across the street to her car, forcing herself not to look back over her shoulder at the man she'd left standing beneath the tree. James Townsend was too tempting, too handsome, too special. He made it so difficult to walk away. All the more reason she had to do so.

KELLY WAS RIGHT. James could find other women willing to bear his child. But the price would be marriage.

That's why his plan had seemed so perfect. Neither of them would have to marry, yet they would have a child to share.

And she'd refused.

James stood and followed Kelly's path across the street to his car. With his hands in his pockets, his head down, he was scarcely aware of those around him. His plan *was* perfect. He just had to find a way to convince her.

And he would.

KELLY RETURNED TO WORK, but her mind refused to deal with advertising campaigns. It was filled with thoughts of the baby she and James could have. Already she'd pictured the child, a little girl, with James's blue eyes, his stubborn chin, her auburn hair. She'd be a charmer, and Kelly would have to work hard not to spoil her.

Only now, when she pictured that precious baby, she couldn't dismiss James from the picture. He'd be beside her, hovering over the crib, stroking a soft cheek.

She'd gotten too close to him, too involved. It was just as well that she'd had to turn him down. Creating a child together would only increase the intimacy and the attraction.

Kelly gave a harsh laugh. Making love with James Townsend would be a glorious experience, she felt sure, but it would be one that she might find impossible to walk away from.

To break the hold his memory had on her, she reached for her purse and the card she'd carried around for over a week. Punching out the number written on the card, she waited impatiently for an answer.

"Family Options. May I help you?"

"Yes, please. My name is Kelly Abbott. I'd like to make an appointment to—to discuss your services."

Five minutes later, when she hung up the phone, she had an appointment in two days and a lot more confidence in her choice. She was going to do what was necessary to save her grandmother. She was going to have a child.

And she could put James Townsend behind her.

After a brief tap on her door, Tex wandered into her office.

"Hey, there, Kel, how's it goin'?"

"Fine, Tex," she assured him, pasting on a smile to hide any remnants of concern.

"Good, good. How'd the meeting go on the Baker project yesterday?"

Relieved that she could report some progress somewhere, Kelly rallied her spirits and said enthusiastically, "Oh, great. We nailed down a dynamite concept. Now we just have to execute it."

"Glad to hear it. Think Bill Howell could carry on without you, since you've got the concept?"

Kelly instantly became alert, shoving away all other thoughts. She knew Tex Warner well. He was avoiding her eyes. That was a sure sign something was up. "Probably. He's coming along quite well."

"Good. See, I've got a little problem with another account, and I'd like you to work on it for me. You could still check in with Bill from time to time." He cleared his throat. "Will you do that for me?"

"What account, Tex?" she asked, but Kelly was afraid she already knew.

Confirming her fears, Tex looked at her for the first time. "The Townsend account."

When she said nothing, Tex prodded her. "You have a problem with that?"

"No. Not if that's what you wish. But—but James and I—that is, we've gone out once socially, and I don't like to mix business and pleasure."

"You intend to keep seein' him?"

"No! Absolutely not."

"So you think his reasons for wanting you on the account are personal and not business?" Tex was studying her closely when she looked at him.

"I don't know."

"He said he was impressed with your conversation with George Canfield. By the way, I talked to Canfield today, and I think he's goin' to be a great customer. There'll be a bonus for you on that one."

"Thanks." She studied her nails, hoping Tex would decide not to put her on James's account.

"About Townsend... I won't insist you handle things for him if you think he's not serious about the job. Or if he's harassing you in any way." Another pause. "Is he?"

Kelly couldn't bring herself to complain about James. "No, I guess not."

"Well, I'd like to keep him happy. So I'm putting you in charge of the Townsend account. But if he gets out of line even one little bit, you let me know. The only thing we're offerin' is advertising. Right?"

"Right," she assured him, forcing a smile.

Tex flicked her cheek and gave her a big smile. "That's my girl. I'll talk to you later." He strolled from the office as casually as he'd entered.

Kelly sighed. So much for avoiding Townsend in the future. The man had just made that impossible.

Ah, well, she'd just have to keep everything on a business level. James Townsend might be her client, but he'd never be the father of her baby. Right.

KELLY NERVOUSLY straightened the silk handkerchief in her breast pocket. After Tex's announcement a few days ago, she'd dreaded her meeting with James. As she'd expected, he'd wanted immediate consultation with the advertising team, but today was the first opening they'd had.

Her telephone rang.

"Mr. Townsend is here, Kelly."

"Thanks, Paige. Show him into the conference room and notify the others."

She rolled her shoulders, trying to ease the tension, and picked up a fresh pad and pen. This meeting was to discuss James's advertising ideas. Her job was to listen.

She could do that—from across the room. James Townsend was too potent at close range. In spite of her resolve, the man had stayed in her mind.

Delaying her entrance until she was sure someone else was present, Kelly walked into the conference room and steeled herself to meet James again.

"Hello, Mr. Townsend," she said, extending her hand and dropping her gaze to his designer tie.

His large hand enclosed hers and didn't let go. "Kelly, it's nice to see you again." He waited until she reluctantly looked at him. "Please, make it James."

His smile invited her to laugh at her ridiculous formality. But she didn't feel like laughing. She felt like running away. With only a nod, she introduced the others who would be working on his ads.

"Shall we get started? Mr. Townsend, if you'll sit—" She stopped because he had circled the table and had his hand on the seat next to her. She tried again. "I think you'll have a better view of our ideas if you sit—"

"I want to sit here, next to you, Kelly. After all, we'll be working closely together."

She glared at him, hoping her colleagues didn't suspect any hidden meaning in his words. "Very well."

Everyone sat down and Kelly cleared her throat. The warmth of James's body as he leaned toward her, the scent of his after-shave, the look in his eyes, made speech almost impossible. All she could think about was the one time he'd kissed her. What was wrong with her?

Just as they started the meeting, the door opened and Tex Warner entered the room. "Everyone here?"

Kelly and the rest of her team stared at their boss. He never bothered to sit in on their meetings unless there was a problem or the client was particularly important. James's account was a healthy one, but it wouldn't make or break their firm. She was afraid her hesitancy in taking the account was the reason for his appearance. She waited for Tex to say something.

"I've got a few free moments. Thought I'd sit in on your meeting. Okay with you, James?"

With an easy grin, James Townsend nodded, but Kelly sensed some tension in his body.

"Do you want to conduct the meeting, then, Tex?" she asked, though she kept her eyes on James.

"No, you go right ahead, Kelly. I'll just watch."

Looks were exchanged by the team members, but Kelly ignored them.

"All right, then, I'll just continue. Mr. Townsend, why don't you tell us what kind of campaign you have in mind for launching your product line into the retail arena?"

At least if James was talking, she wouldn't have to.

The next half hour could only be described as intense torture. At every opportunity James touched her hand, her arm. He implied a closeness in their relationship that went beyond business, in spite of the glares Kelly sent his way.

When the meeting finally came to a close, he shook hands with everyone, but he kept a hand on Kelly's arm. She had intended to escape at the first opportunity, but he must have read her mind. She had to fight to control her responses as she felt the warmth of his fingers on her skin.

They moved toward the exit with everyone else, as if they intended to leave the room. As soon as the last person in front of them walked out, James quietly closed the door.

"What are you doing?" Kelly gasped, trying to pull her arm from his grasp.

"I didn't think you'd see me any other way. What am I supposed to do?"

"Leaving me alone would seem appropriate." Her voice was cold, but her cheeks were hot. James longed to trail kisses over them.

"I can't do that. You started something with your—your request."

"And you finished it with your refusal," she returned, staring straight ahead.

"But I didn't refuse," he insisted even as he leaned closer to her. "At least, my last answer wasn't a refusal. Was it?"

"Yes, it was," she whispered fiercely. "You rejected *my* proposal."

James took her other arm and squared her around to face him. "Look at me, Kelly. It's not fair to just walk away after what's happened between us."

"Nothing has happened between us!" she exclaimed before clamping her teeth into her bottom lip.

He stared at her lips and Kelly nervously looked away. How he'd love to kiss her worries away.

"Have dinner with me one more time. If we can't work out something then, I promise I won't bother you again," he said. He didn't want to make that promise, but he had to buy himself one more chance to have her in his life, at least for a while.

She stared up at him, her green eyes dark with emotion. "You—you promise?"

Unable to resist temptation any longer, he pulled her against him and let his lips take hers. Instead of satisfying his hunger, her mouth only made him want more. More touch, more closeness, more Kelly.

He was so buried in his senses, in Kelly, he didn't hear the door opening behind him. Tex's voice separated them.

"Well, it's a good thing the lady seems to be cooperatin', James, or I'd have your hide stretched up on the wall for a souvenir. However, the office isn't the place for these shenanigans. Right, Kelly?" The sternness of his voice was belied by a twinkle in his eyes.

"My fault, Tex." Nothing less than the truth. He reluctantly dropped his arm from her shoulders. Her kiss said she didn't object to his touch, but her eyes told a different story.

He gathered his papers and pushed open the door. His gaze impaled Kelly—and his words were meant to be suggestive.

"I'll be in touch, Kelly."

In more ways than one, he thought. He had to come up with a plan Kelly would agree to. Either that or take a lot of cold showers.

Chapter Seven

All afternoon, Kelly wanted to call James and cancel their dinner.

But by six-thirty she was walking out of the office to meet him at the restaurant. Just as she was doing so, the phone rang. She almost didn't answer it, afraid it would be James wanting to pick her up. But it was Mary.

"Elizabeth just wanted me to call and find out where you would be in case she needed you."

Kelly stared at the telephone receiver in surprise before putting it back to her ear. Gran had never made this request before. "Well, of course, Mary. I'll be at the Riviera."

James had picked another expensive restaurant famous for its French cuisine.

"Ooh, I've heard that's a nice restaurant. What, Elizabeth?"

Kelly waited, tensing again, expecting, perhaps even hoping, that Gran would need her at home.

"Elizabeth asked if you were going to dinner with that nice Mr. Townsend. I'm sorry to ask, Kelly, but Elizabeth wants to know. I don't mean to pry, you know, but—"

Kelly interrupted Mary's never-ending apology. "It's all right, Mary. Yes, I'll be with Mr. Townsend. We had a meeting today and he asked that we continue the discussion over dinner."

She felt a little guilty about the lie, but she didn't want Gran to worry.

Mary apparently put her hand over the receiver to relay the message to Elizabeth. Kelly, waiting patiently, heard the end of her grandmother's response when Mary took her hand from the receiver. It sounded like "just like that soap opera."

"What did Gran say, Mary?"

"What? Oh, um, she was telling me about a television show she watched today. I gotta go, Kelly. Elizabeth's waiting for her dinner. You have fun now."

Why would Gran be talking about a television program when she'd just asked about Kelly's plans? Was her mind growing more feeble as well as her body?

Kelly was more depressed than ever at that thought. Gran had become weak physically, but her mind had been sharp. Now Kelly was afraid her depression was taking its toll. She was grateful for her appointment tomorrow at the sperm bank. It was important that she not waste time.

When she reached the restaurant, Kelly hesitated at the entrance, nervous at facing James again. Her resolution to keep her distance had crumbled at his touch, which explained why she was dining with him this evening. She had to be stronger, to refuse to give in to the hunger and yearning that filled her when she was near him.

Reminding herself that tomorrow she would be taking the first step in resolving her difficulty without James, she took a deep breath and approached the maître d', giving him James's name. She was immediately shown to a table near the silk-draped windows. James stood as she approached, a warm smile on his lips. He drew the looks of several women seated near him—not surprising since he was an impressive man. That was one of the reasons she'd chosen him in the first place.

After they were seated, he took her hand in his. "I was afraid you wouldn't come."

She looked down at the gleaming china. "I had to work late, that's all."

"So my secretary said." He still held her hand, even when she tugged on it, hoping to distance herself from him.

"I need to read the menu," she said, and he finally released her. She opened the menu and laid it on the table, afraid he would see it tremble if she held it.

"How's your grandmother?" James asked.

Kelly recalled the telephone conversation with Mary, but she'd never reveal her despair to James. "About the same," she lied.

He ran a finger over her hand as it lay on the table, as if he couldn't resist touching her. "You haven't done anything about your idea yet, have you?"

Her gaze flew to his and then away. "I've made an appointment to discuss my options."

"Am I no longer an 'option,' Kelly?" His gaze traveled over her face, caressing it, and lit on her hand.

She pulled her hand into her lap and looked down at the menu. "Not unless you're willing to walk away."

"No decent man would do that."

His absurd statement took her out of her self-consciousness. "James, I could find a thousand women in Dallas alone who could prove otherwise."

"So why didn't you ask one of those men to father your child?" he snapped, irritation on his face.

With a sigh, she smiled ruefully at him. "Because I wanted the best father for my baby."

He shook his head, but his blue eyes showed his appreciation of her words. "Damn, you make it hard to be irritated with you."

"So do you," she retorted. "I should be furious with you for manipulating me into working on your ad campaign, just so you could force me into seeing you."

"That's not the only reason. You're good at what you do, and I like to work with the best."

"How would you know?"

"Because I watched you in action with George. And my opinion was confirmed in the meeting today. You've got a lot of talent."

"Thank you." She was pleased at the compliment but she couldn't resist chiding him on his behavior. "I wasn't sure your mind was on business in the meeting. I don't think that's a very professional way to conduct your affairs."

The grin on James's face alerted her to her poor choice of words. She held up her hand. "Don't say it," she pleaded with despair. "You know what I mean."

"Yeah, but I kind of like the way you phrased it."

The waiter returned to take their order and Kelly chose the first item on the menu. She'd barely looked at the menu but certainly didn't want to prolong the intimacy of their meal by asking for more time to study the selections.

James continued his verbal assault as soon as the waiter left.

"Can't you see what a terrific kid we'd have, Kelly? We're both attractive people, we're bright, we can provide all the necessary things a child needs. All you have to do is agree, and your baby will be the best-loved baby in the world."

She shook her head. "James, my child will be well loved in any case."

"Have you thought about what happens when your grandmother recovers?"

"What do you mean?"

"Regardless of whatever happens to your grandmother, you're going to be left to raise a child on your own." When she would have protested, he silenced her. "I'm not saying your grandmother might die. For all I know, she could live another twenty years. But a grandmother doesn't have the responsibility a mother—or a father—does."

"I'll manage."

"I'm sure you will, but I also know you want what's best for your child."

"Stop it, James. I can't take any more of this. We're going around in circles."

"I know, Kelly," he said, leaning toward her, the blue of his eyes deepening with emotion. "But I have a plan. Will you let me explain?"

How could she say no? She wanted to. She wanted to put her hands over her ears, close her eyes and pretend she was at home, in the den with Gran, and had never approached James Townsend with her question.

"Okay, what's your plan?"

"We just don't tell your grandmother."

Kelly stared at him, stunned by his suggestion. "What?"

He took her hand in his again. "It's simple. We don't tell your grandmother that I'm the father of your child. But I still get to see him, to be there when he's born."

She made no response, still staring at him.

"Your grandmother isn't going to go to the hospital with you when you go into labor. She's in no condition to do that. After the baby is born, you can bring him to my place, say, once a week. I'll even keep him while you shop or run errands. You'll have a built-in baby-sitter.'' He smiled at her as if he'd told an amusing anecdote.

"And just how long do you think we can keep up such a charade?'' she demanded.

"As long as we need to.'' His expression turned serious. "Kelly, your grandmother isn't going to live forever. But if your plan works, then she'll be in good enough health to learn that your child actually does have a father.''

She couldn't argue with his logic. But she also couldn't agree. "I'm sorry, James, but I don't think your plan will work.'' In fact, she knew it wouldn't. And the more time she spent with James Townsend, the more convinced of that she became.

"Why not?'' he snapped, frowning.

"It just wouldn't.''

"That's not a good enough reason, Kelly. You owe me more of an explanation than that.''

The waiter brought their salads to the table, giving Kelly time to gather her thoughts. She wasn't sure a year would be long enough time to find her composure, but she tried. Somehow, she had to explain to James that she was too attracted to him, too involved already, to have an unemotional relationship with him. Without baring her poor heart to him.

"Well?'' he prodded after the waiter had disappeared.

"James, you've asked me to work on your ad campaign. I agreed to do so because I thought our—our personal business had been concluded. I can't take myself off the campaign without giving Tex a good reason. And I couldn't work with you and sleep with you at the same time."

"You think corporate America doesn't share more than a boardroom? Come on, Kelly, you can't be that naive."

"Corporate America can do whatever it pleases, James, but I have no intention of combining those two activities."

"Damn it, Kelly, you make it sound like you're choosing summer camp activities. We're talking about having a child."

She briefly closed her eyes and then looked directly at him. Gone was the comfortable, relaxed man she'd first joined. He was angry, disturbed. "James, you don't have to announce it to the entire restaurant."

He lowered his voice, but he wasn't any happier. "You're telling me that we can't have a child because you're working on my ad campaign? Fine, I'll take my business elsewhere!"

"You can take your business anywhere you please, James Townsend, but you're not going to be the father of my child."

"Why the hell not? I want you, I want our child, I want—"

"My plan isn't about my wants or yours," she interrupted. "It's about my grandmother."

He leaned back in his chair and drew a deep breath. Kelly appreciated his attempt to relax, but she'd rather just leave. Much more probing and he might discover how dangerously near she was to falling in love with him.

"Kelly," he began, his voice gentled, "I know that. But that doesn't mean we couldn't both benefit from the plan. Why would that be so wrong?"

Finally she realized she would have to be honest with him. At least partially. The man wanted her child. But he wanted nothing to do with marriage. Or emotions. Which was only fair, since that was what she'd offered him. *She* had changed, not him.

"James, if you had agreed to my plan that first evening, I—I think I could have carried it off. But it's too late. You see, I don't want to feel anything for the father of my child. I don't want emotions to intrude. And we've spent too much time together. I can't pretend you're a stranger. I can't have sex with you and not want more than you're willing to give. That's why we can't have a child together. You only want the child. I would want more."

She couldn't meet his eyes, afraid she'd see pity in them. She wasn't in love with him. She wasn't! But she could be. She didn't need that kind of misery.

Without another word, she picked up her purse and left him sitting at the table. She didn't think he'd follow her. She'd explained the difficulty too well.

HE MIGHT HAVE TRIED to stop her if he hadn't been so stunned by her words and her departure. James Townsend had never been walked out on before. Betrayed, yes. But not walked out on.

The waiter finally awakened him from his stupor.

"Sir? Your dinner is ready." He didn't mention the absence of the lady, but his gaze traveled to the empty seat opposite James.

"Just bring me the check," James growled.

"Yes, sir."

Once he'd paid the bill, James left the restaurant, eager for the anonymity darkness would give him. He didn't relish people staring at him, pitying him because his date had left him sitting at the table. He'd received enough pity when he'd divorced his wife. Apparently a lot of people had known about her affair even if he didn't.

By the time he reached his apartment, most of his anger had disappeared, leaving a hollow feeling in him. For several days, he'd been concentrating on Kelly and her strange request. His plans for the future had changed.

Now it was as if she had never asked him that question. Because there would be no baby, at least not his baby. That much was clear.

He would have no reason to see her, touch her, again. In fact, if he were wise, he'd be grateful.

So why didn't he feel relieved?

KELLY ENTERED the offices of Family Options with her heart in her throat. Her "other" option was now her only option.

She should have known she wouldn't be able to sleep

with a man she admired without becoming too... attached. She always grew attached to anyone she admired, spent time with. Gran said it was because she'd lost so much at an early age, everyone from her parents to her dog.

It had been a long time since she'd thought about Trudy, the little Lhasa apso her mother had gotten her after her father left. When her mother had been killed in the accident, she and Trudy had come to live with her grandparents. But her grandfather was highly allergic to animal hair.

A neighbor had taken the dog for them, and Kelly had been able to play with her after school. But a year later, that family was transferred to Atlanta, and Trudy had gone with them.

Her heart had been broken.

She was fighting desperately to avoid an even bigger heartache now.

"May I help you?"

Snapped from her depressing thoughts, Kelly greeted the pleasant receptionist and gave her name. At once she was shown into a soothingly decorated office, designed to put one at ease with its soft blue-and-ivory color scheme. The woman behind the desk stood and offered her hand.

"Miss Abbott, please, have a seat. I'm delighted to meet you."

"Thank you, Mrs. Wilcox."

Without further ado, the woman began going over the procedure the clinic followed, and Kelly was both impressed and relieved at the professionalism of the organization.

"Do you have any questions?"

"No, I believe you've covered everything."

"Good. The first step is a physical. You can go to your own doctor or our staff doctor."

"Your staff doctor is fine."

"Very well. Please follow me."

Kelly was relieved to discover the staff doctor was female also. Her own doctor was an old family friend and she'd rather not reveal her plans to her.

The examination was over quickly, and the doctor assured her she was in perfect health.

"Now, Kelly, your most fertile period began yesterday. Unfortunately, because of our scheduling and the paperwork, we'll have to wait until next month before we attempt fertilization."

"Oh, no! Can't we go ahead today?"

The doctor looked surprised at her eagerness, but shook her head no. "I'm sorry, but that's impossible." She patted Kelly's shoulder. "Don't worry. You're a wonderful candidate. I'm sure you'll be successful right away."

Kelly followed the doctor back to Mrs. Wilcox's office and waited for the next step. The director gave her some forms to fill out. In addition to insurance and family history, there were questions about the characteristics she wanted in the birth father.

When she had completed the forms, she handed them over to Mrs. Wilcox and sat back, suddenly feeling drained.

"My, you certainly are definite about your requirements."

Kelly raised her head in surprise. "I beg your pardon?"

"Some of our prospective mothers are a little hazy about the physical requirements of the birth father, as long as he's attractive, athletic and so forth, but you've been quite specific. Six feet two inches, blue eyes, dark hair, a strong chin. It's almost as if you're describing someone you know."

Almost.

Kelly felt like crying.

Chapter Eight

Elizabeth Abbott was already awake when she heard her granddaughter's footsteps on the stairs the next morning. She was anxious to see her.

Kelly opened the door and tiptoed inside, balancing the breakfast tray in her hands.

"Good morning, dear."

"Oh! Good morning, Gran. I didn't know you were awake."

"You got in late last night, so I didn't see you." She watched Kelly as she set down the tray on the end of the bed and turned to put an extra pillow behind her grandmother's back.

"Yes, I went back to the office after dinner. We've got several new clients and I wanted peace and quiet to work on some concepts."

Elizabeth noted that Kelly didn't look at her while she made her explanation. That was a sure sign that something was wrong. Kelly was always straightforward.

"Were you working on Mr. Townsend's account?"

The tray rattled as Kelly transferred it to Elizabeth's lap. "Yes, his account was one of them. Also, we got a new account just a couple of days ago. Mr. Townsend introduced me to George Canfield. He's an old friend of Mr. Townsend's father, and he's decided to use our firm."

Aha! George Canfield. Elizabeth tucked the name into her memory as a squirrel would hide a nut for the winter. Now all she had to do was find a friend who knew George Canfield, get an introduction and then question him about James Townsend.

She couldn't ask Tex any more questions without messing things up for Kelly at work. Tex was already curious. He'd called yesterday to check on her, he said, but *she* thought he was checking on Kelly.

"Gran? Are you all right?" Kelly's anxious voice broke into her thoughts.

"Yes, of course, child," she replied absentmindedly. Perhaps Mildred Potts would know George Canfield. She had always entertained for her husband's business. Yes, she'd call Mildred.

She felt Kelly's kiss on her cheek and looked at her in surprise. Was she leaving already? Good, Elizabeth had things to do.

"Just hang on, Gran. I'm going to make things all right . . . just as soon as I can."

Kelly had already turned to go, but Elizabeth, confused by her granddaughter's words, still noted her pale cheeks. Had Kelly already lost her heart to that schemer, James Townsend? Elizabeth would do anything to keep Kelly from being hurt. The child had already suffered so many losses in her life.

As soon as Mary arrived, they would plan a luncheon and invite Mildred Potts to join them. There was no time to waste.

THERE WAS NO TIME to waste. Kelly felt sure her grandmother's condition was worsening. She'd scarcely been aware of Kelly's presence by the time she'd said goodbye.

But she had to wait another month. She'd hoped they could go ahead with the procedure. If she were waiting to see if they were successful, perhaps she wouldn't think about James Townsend so much.

Yeah, right.

She entered her office, grabbed her cup and filled it from the communal coffeepot down the hall, then went back to her desk. She needed the caffeine. Which only reminded her of James. Damn him! Was he going to haunt her the rest of her life?

Of course not. As long as she avoided him, he'd fade from her memory. Because she didn't love him. Not yet. She hadn't crossed that fatal line, had she?

She wearily rubbed her eyes, tired of the endless debate that she couldn't seem to dismiss, and took another sip of coffee. When the phone rang, she almost dropped her cup.

"Aren't you going to answer it?" Linda asked, stopping in her doorway.

"Would you get it for me? Tell them I'm not in yet?" Kelly asked, hating her cowardly behavior but unable to face whoever was on the other end of the line.

"Kelly Abbott's office," Linda said after picking up the receiver. "Oh, hello, Mr. Townsend. Kelly's not in yet. May I help you? I was in the meeting the other day also. This is Linda Vinson."

Kelly's knuckles whitened as she gripped the coffee mug. Somehow she'd known it would be James on the phone. When she'd finally entered the house last night, Mary told her he'd called several times and would like her to call him when she got in.

As soon as the housekeeper left, Kelly had taken the phone off the hook.

"Oh. I see. Certainly I'll tell her," Linda said before hanging up the receiver.

"My, my, my. You and Mr. James Townsend. You've got great taste, Kelly," Linda teased, waltzing over to her side. "If I thought I had a chance with that hunk, I'd tell Eric to get lost." Since Eric, her husband, was normally compared to a superhero, Kelly didn't take her seriously.

"What did he say?"

"Just that he wasn't calling about the ads. It was a *personal* phone call and please call him as soon as you were free."

"Thanks, Linda," she muttered, rubbing her forehead even as she swallowed the last of her coffee.

"Hey, are you all right? Anything I can do?"

"Yeah, ask the receptionist to hold all my calls. I've got a lot of work to do."

Linda gave her a strange look, but Kelly didn't care. She couldn't face anyone this morning—least of all James Townsend. The last thing she wanted was a postmortem of their disastrous dinner last night.

JAMES HUNG UP the phone in frustration. Kelly was making it perfectly clear that she wanted nothing more to do with him. He didn't care. In spite of his conclusion that Kelly Abbott was out of his life, he couldn't give up. He couldn't stop thinking about her.

After going over her words again and again, he wanted an explanation. What did she mean? Was she telling him she loved him? She certainly hadn't used those exact words. He thought she was saying that they'd become friends, and friends didn't sleep together.

But she was wrong.

Not about their being friends. He agreed. Since their first dinner together, he'd gotten to know Kelly Abbott—and he liked what he'd seen. She was intelligent, honest, unwilling to use her sex to get what she wanted. She liked people. And she would love her child with all her heart.

Everything about her was the opposite of his ex-wife. Except her beauty. Denise had been beautiful, but he'd come to realize, in the end, that her beauty was cold, empty, a shell to lure unsuspecting men.

Kelly's beauty was warm, generous, inviting. If he held Kelly in his arms, he thought he'd never be cold again. As a friend, of course, he hurriedly assured himself.

That's why he needed to talk to her. Friendship would be the perfect relationship for two people having a child. Love wasn't reliable. It involved emotion, a messy, uncontrollable thing that hurt. Friendship was different.

He just had to convince Kelly of that.

After several more tries throughout the morning, James realized Kelly wasn't going to give him the opportunity to convince her of anything. How long did she think she could shut him out?

He flew out the door. If he had to camp on her doorstep to see her, he would. But one way or another, he'd talk to her.

"I'll be out of the office for a while, Liz. Postpone my appointments." His secretary looked stunned as he strode past her desk. For the first time in several years, business wasn't his first priority.

Lunch with some of her office mates relaxed Kelly somewhat. She could isolate herself from James and put him out of her mind. He only intruded when a dark-haired man passed by, or someone mentioned caffeine, or she touched anything plastic or—

"Kelly, there's someone here to see you," the receptionist informed her as she walked through the outer offices, snapping her from her misery. And then doubling it.

James Townsend rose from a chair blocked from her view by a big potted plant.

"J-James!"

"Kelly," he replied, staring at her.

"Are you here to see Tex?" she asked hopefully, saying a silent prayer for his agreement.

"No, I'm here to see you."

"I'm afraid we don't have anything worked up to show you yet, so it would be a waste of your time to meet now." Her voice sounded breathless, but she couldn't do anything about it. She was amazed she was able to speak at all.

"Oh, I don't think our meeting will be a waste of time." His steady regard was unnerving, particularly with the avid audience, made up of her friends from the office, watching the two of them.

"Really, I can't—"

"Do you want to have our discussion out here?" he asked calmly, his gaze going to the others and back to Kelly.

Without another word she turned and led the way down the corridor to her office. She had no doubt that James Townsend would be right behind her.

At her office, he closed the door. She didn't object. After all, she didn't want their discussion flowing down the halls of Bauer, Tate & Warner.

She took the seat behind her desk and gestured to the couch across from it. At least he couldn't touch her from there. With a deep breath, she said, "Actually, James, I'm going to ask Tex to reassign me, so we really don't have anything to discuss."

"I think we do."

She already knew about his determination. Or maybe she should call it stubbornness. But this time, she wasn't going to give in.

"James, I thought I explained the situation last evening. Any—any liaison between us would be impossible."

"You said we couldn't have a child together because we weren't strangers. I disagree."

He leaned toward her and even with the desk between them, she drew back. The last thing she wanted was his touch. She'd already discovered she had little resistance to the warmth that filled her when James Townsend put his hands on her.

"Just listen to me, Kelly." he said.

She bit her bottom lip, trying to forestall the tears that filled her eyes. How could she explain that she couldn't listen any longer? How could she explain that her heart would break when he only showed interest in the child, and not the mother? That she might even grow jealous of her own child.

"James," she whispered, her eyes closed, "I can't do it. I'm sorry. Sorry I ever asked you to—to father my child. But I've already made other arrangements." She opened her eyes and took one look at his intense blue eyes and then looked away. "I don't think we should see each other again."

"But, Kelly, it's *because* we're friends that everything would work out so well."

She was almost tempted to laugh. James still didn't understand. But she'd already risked her heart too much. She couldn't explain again.

"No, James. It wouldn't work." She stood. "Please leave. I'll have Tex assign your campaign to someone else."

He gave her a hard look, frustration in his eyes, before he, too, rose.

Kelly came from behind her desk to open the door for him. Before she could do so, he pulled her into his arms.

His lips slanted across hers hungrily, and she couldn't deny her response. That was part of the problem. She might be able to dissemble with words, but her body was always honest. And her body wanted James Townsend as much as her heart did. Her hands clutched his shoulders and she trembled against him.

He lifted his lips only a fraction of an inch from hers and muttered, "Damn it, Kelly, this can't be wrong. It feels too good."

Before she could argue with him, assuming she would find the strength to do so, he kissed her again. She felt herself spiraling out of control, as she never had before, losing all track of time or place. All that mattered was James.

When he released her lips this time, he stepped back, dropping his arms from her body, leaving her feeling cold and abandoned.

"When you come to your senses, let me know," he growled and stomped from her office.

"TELL ME, MILDRED, have you ever met George Canfield?" Elizabeth asked casually as she nibbled the salad she had ordered. She and Mary had decided a restaurant would be the best option for lunch with Mildred.

"George Canfield? Do you know George? He's the dearest man, isn't he?"

Elizabeth's gaze met Mary's in triumph before she turned back to Mildred. "I haven't met him, actually. Kelly mentioned that he's a client of her firm now."

"I don't think that man will ever retire. He just insists on— Why, speak of the devil." Mildred waved across the room, and Elizabeth discreetly looked over her shoulder.

A tall, distinguished gentleman stood alone, waiting to be seated. Could this be George Canfield? Henry had always said she should frequent Las Vegas with her luck. It appeared it was still good.

"George? Yoo-hoo!" Mildred called. Elizabeth cringed and looked at Mary in apology.

The man crossed to their table, a pleasant look on his face, and took Mildred's hand. "How nice to see you, Mildred. How's Ken?"

"Just the same as ever. Why don't you join us? You're here alone, aren't you?"

The man certainly couldn't argue with that, Elizabeth thought, amused at the trapped expression on his face. He gave it a good try, however.

"I don't want to intrude. I did so the other day and promised myself I wouldn't do it again."

"That must've been when you met my granddaughter," Elizabeth said gently and extended her hand. "I'm Elizabeth Abbott. Kelly told me she'd met you while lunching with—" She paused, as if trying to recall the name.

"James Townsend. You're Kelly's grandmother?" he asked, even as he pulled out the chair next to her. "You don't look old enough to be anyone's grandmother."

Such flattery was ridiculous, of course, but Elizabeth was glad she'd decided to go to the beauty shop before coming to lunch. She introduced Mary and then brought the conversation back to the most important subject.

"Yes, that's right. James Townsend. I believe he's one of Kelly's clients."

George chuckled. "Well, I don't want to spill the beans on Kelly, but my guess is there's a lot more going on there than just business. If I'd realized it before I sat down, I wouldn't have intruded, I promise you. James is a favorite of mine and I'd like to see him happy."

"You've known him a long time?"

"Practically all his life. His father and I have been friends for years."

Perfect. And ridiculously easy. She proceeded to pump George Canfield for all the information she could. He was a pleasant companion, easy to talk to. Like her Henry.

"Tell me, George, is James as big a flirt as you?"

Chapter Nine

"Tex, may I see you?" Kelly asked, sticking her head past the door to his office.

"Sure, Kelly, come on in." Though he waved her in, Tex kept his chair tilted back and his boots on the desk. It was his normal working position.

As much as she dreaded the talk, Kelly had decided not to waste any time.

"What's up, honey?"

She faced him, holding on to her courage, and said, "I need to be removed from the Townsend account."

His gaze never left hers as he lowered his chair to the floor and removed his boots from the desk top. "Let me understand this. Just two days ago, I rearranged almost the entire office just so you could be put on the Townsend account—with your approval, I might add—and now you want off? You'd sure better have a dadgum good reason."

She studied her clenched hands in her lap before looking at him again. "James and I have some per-

sonal conflicts that will make working with him difficult."

"Personal conflicts? From what I interrupted yesterday, I can believe it's personal, but I didn't see much
conflict."

With great concentration, she kept the tears in her
eyes from falling. "It's a conflict now."

"Did he get too, you know, friendly? I'll have his
hide if he did."

"No, Tex. Truly. It's just a personal problem."

Tex studied her a minute more before leaning across
the desk. "Well, now, see, honey, it's this way. After
all the rearranging I did, you brought in the Canfield
account and I had to stretch us a bit more. I don't have
anyone else to put in charge of James's advertising."

She stared at him in dismay. "No one? How about
Bill Casing?"

"He's on the Hudson account, the Newberg account and is assisting on the Clark account."

"Linda? Isn't she ready to take charge of an account?"

"Kel, she's just not ready. I'm planning on startin'
her on something smaller, anyway. Whatever the
problem you're having with James, you know how
important this campaign will be to his new retail ven-
ture."

She nodded glumly.

"Can't you do the work, and when the presentation
comes around, I'll stick to your side like glue. Okay?"

Since she didn't think she had a choice without leaving Tex in a lurch, she nodded again and slipped from his office. The day had been rolling downhill since it started, and now it was picking up steam.

After checking with Mary, Kelly stayed at the office late, working on James's account. The sooner she made the presentation, the sooner she could put the man out of her life. But she made sure she left the office in time to visit with Gran before she went to bed.

But when she got home, at seven forty-five, Gran had already gone to bed.

"But why, Mary? It's much earlier than usual."

"Well, I—I took her out in the car for just a little while today. You said I could, you know. But I think it tired her out."

Kelly was touched by the guilty look on Mary's face. What a kind woman she was, caring for Gran as she did. What would Kelly do without her?

"Thanks, Mary, for trying to help her take an interest in something. Don't worry about it. Maybe tomorrow she'll want another ride." She turned to go up the stairs. "I'll just check on her. She might not be asleep yet."

Without waiting for an answer, she hurried to her grandmother's bedroom. Sometimes Gran had difficulty going to sleep even though she was tired. Tonight wasn't one of those times. Gran was lying on her side, gently snoring.

She was closing the door again when the shaft of light fell on the bedside table. A vase of red roses,

Gran's favorite flowers, stood there. Granddad used to send them to her on special occasions. Where had they come from?

When she returned downstairs, Mary was waiting to leave.

"Is she all right?"

"She's sleeping like a baby. How does she seem to you, Mary? Did she take an interest in what she saw today?"

Mary's cheeks were flushed, and Kelly wondered if she'd gotten overtired taking care of Gran. "She—she seemed pleased."

"Good."

Still Mary didn't leave.

"Is anything wrong, Mary?"

"No, not wrong. That is, Elizabeth asked me about moving in here with the two of you. To take care of her in the evenings so you can go out when you feel like it."

Kelly sank down into a chair at the breakfast table.

"Kelly, what's wrong?" Mary asked, rushing to her side.

"It just seems like she's completely giving up. She doesn't expect to ever get better if she needs round-the-clock care."

"Oh, no! It's not like that. We've become good friends, Kelly. I don't have anyone at home since my husband died, and Elizabeth doesn't want to tie you down. That's all."

"Would you enjoy living here with us?"

Mary looked embarrassed but she nodded yes. "I get lonesome," she added simply.

"Okay. I'll talk to Gran in the morning about it. But you'll have to be sure we don't impose on you," Kelly warned, knowing how warmhearted Mary was.

"As if you would," Mary said and left after saying goodbye, a smile on her face.

Kelly stood there, staring at the back door, wondering whether her grandmother's decision was good or bad. Having Mary there round-the-clock would be helpful for Kelly, if it was what Gran wanted.

Not that she had a big social life. But after the baby was born, Mary would be a big help.

JAMES WAS DISCOURAGED. He'd spent the afternoon trying to work, but thoughts of Kelly intruded. He stared at the phone, longing to call her, to argue his case again.

At least she couldn't have any doubt about their physical compatibility. Their kisses hadn't been one-sided. Frustration rose up in him, and he sighed. He was too old for constant cold showers.

As he entered his apartment, the flashing light on his answering machine caught his eye and he put his brief-case down. Maybe Kelly had called. He tried to ignore the leap his heart took at the thought. Pressing the button, he waited for his messages.

"James, this is Ceci. Give me a call."

Beeeeeep

"Mr. Townsend, this is Dr. Baylor's office. It's time to get your teeth cleaned. Give us a call to set up an appointment."

Beeeeeep

"James, darling, I haven't seen you in weeks. Are you going to call?" Definitely sultry, but not Kelly.

Beeeeeep

"James, this is your mother. Will you call us, please? No emergency, but as soon as you can."

He reached for the phone at once. He and his parents talked regularly, but something in his mother's voice alarmed him.

"Mom, is everything all right?"

"James! Everything's fine."

It was a relief to hear her sounding so cheerful. "Where's Dad?"

"Fortunately, he's— I mean, he's next door playing cards this evening."

He frowned. Were his parents having marital problems? Usually they spent most of their time together. When his mother said nothing else, he asked, "You wanted to talk to me?"

"Oh, yes, well, your father heard from an old friend yesterday. He said he'd visited with you at a restaurant."

Damn George Canfield and his big mouth. James knew what was coming next.

"He said you were with a lovely young woman, Kelly Abbott."

"It was a business lunch, Mom, that's all. She's in charge of my advertising account."

"Yes, that's what George said. But I was curious, because he said she's from Dallas. I met an Elizabeth Abbott several times at the garden club I used to attend with Ceci's mother. Is Elizabeth Kelly's mother?"

James shook his head, a wry smile on his face. His mother could make a connection with a stranger in the Gobi Desert probably inside fifteen minutes. "Elizabeth is her grandmother, Mom. Her parents are dead."

"Oh, the poor dear. Well, the next time we're in town, I'd love to meet Elizabeth again. And Kelly, too, of course."

"Of course," he agreed, knowing to protest would be futile. "She can explain my advertising campaign to you."

"James," Carolyn protested, exasperation in her voice, "can't you show some interest in Kelly? She sounds perfectly wonderful and—"

"Carolyn, are you pestering the boy?" Richard's voice came from a distance.

"Richard! I thought you were playing cards."

Now James understood why his mother was glad his father was next door. He waited while his parents had a whispered discussion not quite loud enough to hear. Then his father came on the line.

"Sorry, son. After George called, your mother has been speculating nonstop. I told her not to bother you."

"It's okay, Dad. I just wish she'd quit worrying about me."

His father chuckled. "That'd be like telling a dog not to bark. That's what mothers do, son."

"Yeah." Kelly would be the same way. She'd let her child make his own way, but she'd worry the entire time. Just like his mother.

"James? You are okay, aren't you? George was afraid he'd horned in where he shouldn't have." Apparently it wasn't only mothers who worried.

"No problem, Dad. It really was a business lunch." He wasn't lying. He just wasn't telling the whole truth. And if he had a son one day, he hoped the child would do the same favor for him. He'd only worry himself to death, like his mother, his father, Kelly and anyone else who cared.

He supposed that was part of loving someone.

He hung up the phone after saying his goodbyes. He'd avoided worrying about anyone the past few years, except his parents, and maybe his sister and his cousin Ceci. But he'd distanced himself from even them. He'd been afraid to care.

After he discovered his wife's betrayal, he'd hidden his heart, hoping to avoid being hurt again. Work had become his life.

Fixing a cup of instant coffee, he wandered around his living room, drinking it, thinking about the change in his life since that fateful night he and Kelly had had dinner together. He'd been like Sleeping Beauty, as silly as that sounded. And Kelly had brought him to life with her question.

Shock therapy.

Just like she intended to use on her grandmother.

"BUT, ELIZABETH, I thought you said George raved about James."

"He did, Mary. He thinks James is wonderful. But he doesn't really know about how the man treats women." Elizabeth drummed her fingers on the table. "What's important is how Kelly feels. You can't tell me you think she looks happy."

Mary frowned. "Well, no, but maybe she's worried about something at work."

"She's worked there for seven years and enjoyed every minute of it. No, it's James Townsend who's making her miserable." Elizabeth stood and paced the kitchen.

Mary felt guilty about letting Elizabeth spend so much of her energy, but like love, it only seemed to increase when it was spent.

"Oh my stars!" Elizabeth exclaimed. "What is that man doing?"

Before Mary could even understand her question, much less give an answer, Elizabeth had pulled open the back door and run outside. She followed to find Elizabeth chastising the gardener.

"Elizabeth, you should come back inside."

"That man's going to kill my prized rosebushes. Why, he knows nothing about pruning them."

"Ma'am, I'm just following instructions," the workman said, backing away from Elizabeth's fierceness.

Before Mary knew what was happening, Elizabeth had fired the gardener and taken up the shears herself.

"Elizabeth, Kelly will kill me if you overdo things. Please come back inside."

"In a minute. I've just got to repair the damage that moron did. My roses are very precious to me." She cast Mary a roguish look. "I can't count on George sending me a dozen roses all the time, now, can I?"

Mary watched her in exasperated silence. They'd both been surprised when the florist had delivered the roses yesterday afternoon. Obviously George Canfield was enchanted with Elizabeth, who had certainly set out to charm him.

It seemed to Mary that Elizabeth was improving daily, turning into an impish, fascinating woman, shedding her years as if they didn't exist. If this is what Elizabeth was like before her husband's death, no wonder Kelly had missed her, worried about her.

"What are you going to do now that you've fired the gardener, Elizabeth? You certainly can't take care of this yard yourself," Mary reminded her.

"No, but I can take care of my rosebushes. And maybe a few of the flower beds. I'll hire someone to do the rest."

Mary stood watching Elizabeth, debating whether she should try to stop her. She wasn't sure she could if she tried.

"Why don't you go put on a pot of tea, Mary, and make us a snack. I'm going to be hungry after I finish this," Elizabeth directed, never looking up from her work.

Mary did as she was bid, all the time wondering who was taking care of whom.

"GOOD MORNING, Mr. Townsend," his secretary greeted him.

"Good morning, Liz. Any messages?"

She handed him his telephone messages and he flipped through them quickly. She hadn't called.

But his cousin had. He dialed her. "Ceci, you called?"

"Oh, James, yes—just a minute." She shrieked and it sounded to James like she dropped the phone. When she spoke to him again, he asked, "Is everything all right?"

"Sure. Just a typical morning. Your nephew was heading for the family room with chocolate milk and peanut butter and jelly."

"Is that bad?" He'd seen the kids eat all kinds of things in Ceci's family room.

"Today it is. I'm cleaning the house for a party."

The premonition James had both pleased and irritated him. Ceci shouldn't butt into his life, but if what he believed was true, he'd have another chance to spend time with Kelly.

"What kind of party?" Since Ceci's husband, Rob, was a stockbroker, they entertained a lot. He could be wrong about her plans.

"I was thinking about having a sort of minireunion with some of my friends."

"You think Rob's anxious to meet all your old boyfriends?" he asked, unable to resist teasing his cousin.

"You know Rob. If he can sell them stocks, he doesn't care what happened in the past." Ceci paused and then added with a mock-casual air, "I thought I'd include Kelly. I'd like to see her again."

"I wonder why that doesn't surprise me?"

"Should I invite you, too? Or have you lost interest in having Kelly work on your advertising?" Her voice hinted for him to come clean about his intentions toward Kelly, but he wasn't about to be honest about what was going on.

"I suppose I could come, if all your old girlfriends are as cute as Kelly. No sane man would pass up such an opportunity."

"I thought maybe Kelly would invite you as her date."

"She probably has a string of men anxious for an invitation," he said, while his brain screamed a silent protest. "In fact, if you want her to come, it might be best not to mention my being invited."

"Did you two have a fight?"

"No, of course not. But some people don't like to associate with business connections after hours." He hoped Ceci didn't know any of Kelly's compatriots at the advertising agency. He'd be lucky if she spoke to him if that was the case. "Just let me know when it is, and I'll put it on my calendar."

"Tomorrow night."

"That's kind of short notice, isn't it?" Maybe that wasn't such a bad idea since it wouldn't give Kelly much time to come up with an excuse. "What time?"

"Seven-thirty. And come casual. We want everyone to feel at ease."

"Right. I'll see you then."

And hopefully, Kelly, too.

THE MOMENT KELLY LEFT work, her mind reverted to her personal problems. Not that she'd avoided them at the office. She had to constantly concentrate to keep James out of her head. He was driving her crazy.

Wearily she closed her office door behind her and walked to the parking lot. She'd promised her grandmother they'd spend some time together this evening, watch TV, talk. Neither required much concentration, something she seemed incapable of lately.

The aroma of roast beef greeted her as she entered the house. Mary had already prepared dinner, thank goodness.

"Gran? I'm home."

She dumped her belongings down on top of the washer and proceeded into the kitchen.

"Hello, dear," Elizabeth greeted her with a smile. "I'm just getting ready to serve our plates. Are you ready to eat?"

"Yes, but where is Mary?"

"Oh, I sent her home early. Since she'll need to spend tomorrow night here, I thought she deserved a little extra time. It will certainly be easier when she's living here with us, won't it?"

Elizabeth's words almost passed over Kelly's head. Then she realized she had no plans for tomorrow night.

"Tomorrow night? Why did you say tomorrow night?"

"Oh, I forgot to tell you. You're going to be so pleased!" Elizabeth beamed at her as she carried several dishes over to the kitchen table.

"I am?" Kelly asked cautiously.

"Yes! Ceci Forrester called today. Oh, that's not her name now, of course, because she married, but—"

"Ceci Evans." Somehow Kelly didn't think she was going to like what her grandmother had to say.

"What? Oh, yes, that's right. Ceci Evans. I didn't know you'd kept up with her, dear. Anyway, she's going to have a party tomorrow night for several old school friends and wanted you to come."

Kelly closed her eyes. The last thing she needed was to see her old friends, be reminded of her failed engagement, hear about everyone's children. "You didn't tell her I'd come, did you?"

"She said you could bring a date," Elizabeth continued, as if Kelly hadn't spoken. "I told her you'd probably come alone, that you really weren't dating anyone right now, since you're spending your evenings working."

"Gran, I don't want to go. Did you say I would?"

With a stubborn look on her face, Elizabeth nodded yes. "It will be good for you, dear. All work and no play, you know. Besides, you need to meet some nice young men."

Kelly almost burst into hysterical laughter. She'd just made the decision to carry out her plan *without* a nice young man.

But the party might be a good idea for another reason. It might take her mind off James. And at this point, she'd do anything for a distraction that was more powerful than the feelings she had for James Townsend.

If such a thing existed.

Chapter Ten

Ceci greeted James at the door. "I didn't think you were ever going to arrive."

"Is Kelly here?"

Though her eyebrows soared, Ceci only said, "Yes, she's in the den."

James followed his cousin to the large family room but the sight of almost thirty people halted him in his tracks. He'd expected about a third that number.

"How many people did you invite?" he demanded under his breath, his eyes searching for Kelly.

"About twenty-five people, but everyone brought a date, except you and Kelly and a few others."

He paid no attention to her response because he'd just found Kelly. Kelly and five or six men. "Didn't *they* bring dates?"

"Who?"

"The men flocked around Kelly."

"Most of them did. Except for Bryan. He came hoping to see Kelly again."

"Which one is he?" He kept his eyes on Kelly, willing her to look at him, but she was talking to a good-looking man standing to her right.

"The one she's talking to, in the green shirt."

His eyes narrowed as he strode across the room, evaluating his competition. As he reached the group, Kelly looked up and he was reassured by the reaction he thought he saw in her eyes. The desire to stake his claim on her with a kiss was taken away from him, however, when she extended her hand to him.

"Mr. Townsend. How nice to see you again."

He was startled by her formality, and also by her lack of reaction to his appearance.

"You're not surprised to see me?" he asked as he took her hand.

"No. Ceci mentioned you when I arrived." The look in her eyes told him she'd wanted to turn around and leave, but she couldn't upset an old friend.

"Bryan, let me introduce James Townsend. I'm working on his ad campaign. Mr. Townsend, this is Bryan Hensen, an old friend. Bryan is living in Austin and is on the Speaker of the House's staff." Kelly then introduced the other men around her, but James couldn't remember their names even as he acknowledged their greetings.

"Nice to meet you, Mr. Townsend," Bryan said, making James feel ancient.

"Please, call me James. I don't think any of us should be formal this evening. Right, Kelly?"

"Of course not—James," she finally said.

"What do you do for a living?" Bryan asked, turning to him after looking at Kelly curiously.

"I have a company that makes plastic products, like the dishes on airplanes."

"Really? Well, I guess I've used your products a lot, then, 'cause I'm always on airplanes." He turned his attention back to Kelly, draping an arm around her shoulders. "Maybe I can give you some help with your ad work, Kelly, since I'm an experienced customer."

"In more ways than one," James muttered under his breath, glaring at the offending arm around Kelly.

"I'm sorry, I didn't hear what you said," Bryan replied, leaning toward James, which drew Kelly closer to Bryan.

"I said I don't think Kelly needs any help."

"A customer's opinion is always valuable," Kelly murmured, smiling at Bryan.

"Oh, James," Ceci called, coming up to them, "there's someone I want you to meet. And you haven't said hello to Rob, either."

She tugged at his arm. After a frustrated glare at her, James turned back to Kelly. "I'll see you later," he muttered, determined to make some kind of claim on her. Kelly only nodded, her eyes wide, as he followed Ceci across the room.

"Is THAT GUY causing you problems?" Bryan asked, his eyes on James.

"What?" Kelly asked, startled.

"You know, harassing you? You should report him if he is. You don't have to put up with that stuff anymore."

Kelly's cheeks flamed and she stared at her hands clenched in her lap. "No. No, James isn't harassing me."

"Well, something's going on between the two of you."

"We just met recently. I guess we're just getting to know each other." She knew James well enough to know he was unhappy with her.

"Watch your step with him. I think he's interested in more than an ad campaign," Bryan growled. He tightened his hold on Kelly's shoulders. "And now that I've found you again, I don't think I want anyone else near you."

The other men seated near them had been discussing sports, but one of them overheard Bryan's remarks and turned to Kelly. "Hey, don't pay any attention to this guy. I've heard he's cut a wide swath through the hearts of the ladies in Austin."

"That's in my past," Bryan protested, smiling when several others hooted in derision.

"He certainly did so in high school," Kelly added, delighted to move the conversation away from herself. "Do you remember when he dated three girls at once and they all caught him with a fourth?"

Over Bryan's protests, his love life in high school dominated the conversation for a while. Kelly pretended an interest she didn't feel and watched James across the room. Whenever their glances met, she felt his anger.

A few minutes later, when several of the men began clearing the floor of furniture under Ceci's direction, James returned. "How about the first dance, Kelly?"

"I don't think I want to dance, thanks anyway," Kelly responded to his request.

He took her hand and tugged her to her feet, ignoring her words. "I want to talk to you. Would you prefer that to dancing?" he whispered as she stood.

She glared at him, before preceding him to the space cleared out.

"Kelly, how about a dance?" Bryan asked, as soon as he finished helping with the rug. He'd been one of the men Ceci recruited.

"Sorry, Bryan. I asked first." James even smiled at the man, when he'd have preferred knocking his teeth in. He couldn't remember the last time he'd felt so juvenile.

"That wasn't very nice," Kelly whispered as she placed her hand on his shoulder.

"I didn't say anything rude," James assured her, pulling her close to him, delighted to have her in his arms again. She fit perfectly against him, his jaw resting against her temple. When she tried to shift away, he held her firmly.

"Relax, we're just dancing."

"I'll step on your toes if we dance this close."

"Then I'll just hold you and we can sway back and forth. No one's expecting Fred and Ginger."

"James!" she whispered warningly.

"Okay, okay," he relented and began to move in time to the music. As long as he got to hold her, he wouldn't complain.

After several minutes of bliss, he whispered, "I've been waiting for you to call me."

"About what?"

"Don't play innocent," he reprimanded, his voice soft as he inhaled her scent, part some flowery perfume and part just Kelly.

"James, that subject is closed. I don't want to discuss it ever again."

A lot of conflicting emotions surged through him. He feared she'd already been impregnated, taking away his chance to father her child. He was concerned for her and the turmoil she was putting herself through. And he was worried about their future.

He wanted Kelly in it.

He'd missed seeing her, talking to her, touching her.

"Oh, Kelly," he said with a sigh, his lips touching her temple.

"Don't—don't be sweet, James, please. Yell at me or refuse to speak to me ever again. But don't be sweet."

He lifted her chin so he could see into her green eyes. When he found them filled with unshed tears, he wrapped both arms around her, cuddling her against him.

"Shh, Kelly, don't get upset." In spite of his frustration with her, he never wanted to hurt her. "I'll help.

I'll be there for you, sweetheart. We're friends, re-member?''

KELLY SHUDDERED against his warm strength. Friends. The man thought they were friends. She gave herself all kinds of lectures while she moved in his arms. If only the music would never stop. But that was the kind of thinking that made her weak.

When the music ended, Bryan was beside them, asking for the next dance. Kelly greeted him with a yes, glad to be separated from James. She couldn't stand being so close to what she couldn't have.

"That guy's got it bad, doesn't he?" Bryan asked, his eyes on James as they moved around the floor.

"What?" Kelly asked, startled.

"You know, got a case on you? How do you feel about him? You looked like you were about to cry. I mean, if he's causing you problems, you should tell him to get lost.''

Kelly's cheeks flamed but she managed a laugh. "Thanks for the advice, but there's no problem. James is . . . is a friend as well as a client.'' Hysterical laughter bubbled up. Now she was giving James's lines.

"Good. So why's he making you cry, then?''

She looked away. "I'm just being silly.''

"Well, just give the word, and I'll beat him up for you,'' Bryan offered, teasing, she thought. But there was a serious note in his voice that left her wondering.

She lifted her head and smiled at him, refusing his offer, but as he turned her about the room, her gaze met James's. He had murder in his eyes as he glared at the two of them.

She hastily changed the subject with Bryan and finished out the dance with a smile on her lips. It was funny, she realized, that Bryan held her as close as James, but she felt perfectly comfortable with him. When James had held her pressed against him, her heart had raced and longing had almost driven her wild.

The music ended and James appeared beside them.

"How about the next dance, Kelly?"

"Sorry, but I promised Tommy the next one," she said impulsively, hoping her old friend wouldn't mind being dragooned into duty. Fortunately, he was sitting alone nearby and responded to her plea not to keep her waiting, even though he looked a little confused.

Again James watched their every move.

Tommy readily accepted Kelly's explanation that she wanted to have time to talk to him alone. His hot breath blew on her neck as he clutched her close to him, but she scarcely noticed.

All she could think about was James's touch.

She was afraid if he held her again, she wouldn't be able to hide the truth she'd just discovered. She loved James Townsend. Her good friend, James Townsend.

Tears welled up in her eyes.

"Did I step on your toe?" Tommy asked worriedly. "I didn't mean to. I haven't done a lot of dancing since high school, you know, so—"

"No, Tommy, you didn't. I was thinking about something sad. Really, it wasn't anything you did."

"Well, can I help you? Do something for you?" he asked.

"Just be my friend, Tommy. That's all."

"Sure. But I'd like to be more than that. Can I give you a call?"

"That's sweet, Tommy, but I'm going to be tied up the next few months with—with someone else. If it doesn't work out, maybe we can get together?"

"Oh. With that Townsend guy?"

"No! No, it's someone you don't know."

"Oh."

When the music ended, James was at her side.

"My dance, I think."

"Sorry, James, but I need to be excused," she said, using the only excuse she could think of. "I'm going to powder my nose."

She hurried to the bathroom, breathless, anxious to be away from his piercing gaze. It was difficult to be in the same room with him, wanting him, knowing all he wanted was friendship. Instead of returning to the den, she sought out Ceci in the kitchen.

"Ceci, I really have to go, but thanks for inviting me."

"Already? But, Kelly, you just got here an hour ago."

"I'm sorry, but I've got to go back to the office and put in another couple of hours."

"Are you sure it's not because James is here?" Ceci asked, an anxious look in her eyes. "I should have warned you, I guess."

"But James told you not to," Kelly guessed. "Has he talked about—about us?"

"A little, but I don't know what's going on between the two of you. Except that something is. Want to talk about it? We could go to lunch together next week." Ceci waited for her response, a welcoming smile on her face.

"There's nothing to talk about. But I'd love to have lunch together sometime. I'll call you in a couple of weeks and we'll catch up on old times."

"Promise?"

"I promise." She kissed Ceci's cheek and headed for the door. "Will you make my goodbyes for me? If I go back in there, I'll never get away."

"Sure. Call me," Ceci reminded her as the door swung to behind her.

Kelly slipped out the front door, relief filling her at not being seen. Why did she have to choose the one man in Dallas, a total stranger, who was kin to one of her old high school friends? Thank goodness they hadn't gone ahead with the pregnancy. She couldn't have looked Ceci in the eye.

Family Options was the right choice.

No identity.

No connections.

No strings attached.

Now, if she could only forget James's touch, his scent, his voice.

His blue eyes.

Chapter Eleven

James stood with his hands in his pockets, his gaze glued to the door of the den. He had no interest in his cousin's other guests. Only Kelly.

After their dance together, he'd felt empty, alone, as he watched her in other men's arms. He'd also felt angry. He didn't want anyone touching her except him. Her body had left an imprint on his that he couldn't forget.

When had she become so important to him?

He couldn't answer that question. He only knew that he couldn't walk away from Kelly, whatever happened about the baby. These past few days, waiting for her to call, had been the longest in his life. He didn't want a future without her.

He was lost in dreams of that future when Rob bumped into him.

"Oops! Sorry, James. Did I get any dip on you?" Rob asked, holding a tray with dip and chips in front of him.

"No, Rob. I didn't mean to block the door. I was just waiting for Kelly." He'd already turned back to watch for her arrival even as he explained.

"Well, you're going to have a long wait. She left." Rob started to walk away but James whirled around and grabbed his arm. "Hey, watch it, James, or I'll have you covered in dip."

"What did you say?"

"I said, watch it—"

"No, about Kelly."

"She left. At least that's what Ceci said. She was disappointed 'cause they didn't get a chance to talk—"

James didn't wait for him to finish but headed to the kitchen to question Ceci. He found her putting ice in more glasses.

"Where's Kelly?"

"She had to leave, said she needed to work."

"Work? She was going to her office?"

"That's what she said." Ceci leaned toward him. "You didn't upset her, did you?"

Upset her? No more than she upset him. His body was throbbing with desire, his nostrils filled with her scent, his head thinking only of her. He hoped he'd had the same effect on her. Without another word, he turned to leave.

"Where are you going?" Ceci called after him.

"I have some work to do, too," he said, never slowing down. And he did. Only, his work involved making connections with a certain warm, passionate redhead, instead of having anything to do with business.

When he reached the dignified old building where Bauer, Tate & Warner had their offices, he almost ran through the lobby, all his thoughts on Kelly.

"Hold up there! This building is closed!"

He turned around to see an elderly security guard sitting behind a small desk. Though he was impatient to find Kelly, James turned around and walked back across the lobby. He read the name badge and remembered hearing some of the employees call him Jake. Jake McDonald.

"Hi, Jake. I forgot you'd be on duty tonight."

The elderly man leaned forward, squinting slightly.

"Do I know you?"

"You probably don't remember me, but I'm one of Bauer, Tate & Warner's clients." He stuck out his hand. "James Townsend, president of Townsend Industries."

"Oh, yes, sir. Well, the building's closed." The man shook his hand with a smile but didn't seem prepared to let him go by.

"Of course, I know. But Kelly Abbott is working late tonight on my account. I just had an idea that I'd like to pitch to her."

The look of recognition that crossed the guard's face relieved James.

"She did say she was going to work when she checked in here a few minutes ago. Well, I guess it'll be all right, but I'll just call up there to be sure."

"No, there's no need to call. It'll just interrupt her twice. She won't mind my coming up."

"I don't know, Mr. Townsend. . . ."

James didn't want Kelly warned of his arrival. She'd probably tell Jake to throw him out. Fortunately, a deliveryman arrived with a load of packages, drawing Jake's attention.

"Isn't it kind of late to be making deliveries?" Jake asked with suspicion.

"I'll just go on up and get out of your way," James muttered and walked quietly toward the elevators. Over his shoulder he saw Jake give a distracted nod as he talked to the deliveryman.

He held his breath until the elevator door closed behind him. If his luck held, the guard would be tied up until he'd already reached Kelly.

The glass door to the advertising agency was unlocked, and he hurried through the dimly lit reception area down the hallway to Kelly's office. Her door was closed but there was a thin stream of light along the bottom. Without knocking, he opened the door.

KELLY HAD TAKEN OFF her jacket, the short-sleeved silk blouse she wore beneath it much cooler, and sat down at her desk. But she'd accomplished nothing.

All she could think about was James.

When he'd held her in his arms, dancing, she'd felt so—so complete, so satisfied and yet so hungry for more. Never in her life had desire taken such a hold on her. Until she thought she'd die if he didn't take her further, touch her more, make her a part of him.

That feeling scared her.

She was only setting herself up for heartbreak. James wasn't willing to give her what she now realized she wanted. She knew he had no intention of marrying again, at least not a marriage where he'd put his heart at risk.

And that was the only kind of marriage she wanted.

One like Gran and Granddad had, one that would last forever.

She covered her face with her hands, weary of the thoughts tormenting her. In the darkness her hands provided, her hearing picked up the slight sound of footsteps on the carpeted hallway floor.

Someone was in the office! Immediately she remembered she hadn't bothered to lock the outer door. Tex always warned them about working late without keeping the door locked.

The footsteps came closer down the hall. Kelly grabbed the phone, frantically trying to remember Jake's extension in the lobby. The door burst open and she forgot to breathe.

James walked into her office.

Relief was so heady, she almost lost consciousness.

"Kelly! Are you all right? What's wrong?"

"What's wrong? You scare me to death and ask what's wrong? How dare you walk in here without warning! I can't believe—"

"Kelly, calm down. I didn't mean to scare you. But if you're that worried about anyone coming in, why did you leave the front door unlocked?"

"That's beside the point! Why are you here?"

"I wanted to—"

The phone beneath her fingers rang, and Kelly jumped again. She was going to have to get control of herself.

"Hello?"

"Kelly, this is Jake. Did Mr. Townsend come up there?"

"Yes, he did."

"Well, is that okay? Do you want me to come escort him out of the building?"

Kelly was tempted. She didn't want to have a private confrontation with James. But better now, when no one was around to hear, than in a crowded restaurant or his condo. "No, Jake, it's okay."

"You sure?"

She lifted her gaze to James's intense blue one, watching her as she talked to the security guard. She wasn't sure, but she couldn't tell Jake that. "I'm sure."

"You call if you need me."

"I will, Jake, and thanks for checking on me." She hung up the phone reluctantly, wishing she could have prolonged it, anything to delay facing James.

To her surprise, however, his eyes didn't hold anger. He gave her a crooked smile and said, "Thanks for vouching for me."

She nodded. "But I don't think it's a good idea for you to be here, James. I'm in the middle of working on your—"

"I'm not here to talk about advertising, Kelly, and you know it."

"But, James—"

"Why did you run out on me?"

There was an unexpected tenderness in his question that unnerved her. Unable to face him, she traced the buttons on the phone with a finger. "I—I needed to come back to work."

"Are you sure you didn't run out because you thought I was going to argue with you again?"

One large hand slid beneath her chin to lift her face to his.

"Weren't you?" she finally asked.

He grinned again, rocking her resistance.

"I'd like to, Kelly Abbott, but I've discovered you're just about as stubborn as me." He waited for her wobbly grin to appear. "I may be stubborn, but I don't beat my head against a brick wall."

At his words, relief filled her that she didn't have to fight him anymore, but on its heels, chasing it away, was the devastating disappointment that he was giving up. He didn't even want her baby anymore.

"I see." She dropped her lashes to cover the despair she felt sure was visible. A trembling seized her as she tried to hide what she was feeling.

His hands caressed her shoulders.

"Sweetheart, what's wrong? Why are you shaking?"

"B-because I'm pleased you understand," she mumbled, hoping he'd buy such a ridiculous response.

He pulled her from behind her desk and led her to the sofa. When he settled the two of them against the cushions, his arm around her shoulders, holding her against him, Kelly thought she would scream. Such torture, his offering so easily the touch she craved.

"But there's something I want you to understand, too," he said, leaning his cheek against her hair.

She was afraid she was beyond all comprehension, but she struggled to concentrate. "What?"

"I'm willing to accept your decision that your way is best, but I can't walk away and leave you to shoulder the burden by yourself." As he talked, he reached down to take her hand in his, his fingers rubbing her knuckles, stroking her palm, encircling her wrist.

In spite of an urge to touch him in return, she pulled away, turning to face him. "What are you saying?"

"Kelly, when Ceci was pregnant, she needed Rob there with her every step of the way. You'll need someone, too. I'm offering to be there for you."

Kelly stared at him, wondering which of them had lost their mind. Didn't he understand that even a pregnant woman wanted more from a man than his friendship? "You can't—"

"Yes, I can. I may not be the father, but I feel responsible. We've formed a special bond, Kelly, just talking about being parents together.'' He pulled her back against him, his lips caressing her forehead. ''Even if I walked away, I wouldn't be able to forget what you're going through.''

Before she could speak, he added, ''And I haven't forgotten about your grandmother. You don't have to tell her I'm around. We'll talk on the phone, meet for dinner occasionally.''

She shook her head in disbelief. Her father had had no problem walking away from her. Her fiancé had betrayed her with scarcely a qualm. But this man, on whom she had no claim, refused to walk away. And his staying, as a friend, would hurt her more than either of the others' departures. In spite of her determination, her eyes filled with unshed tears, even as she looked up at him.

''Oh, sweetheart, don't cry,'' James pleaded softly, his hands caressing her shoulders, pulling her closer to him.

The hard warmth of his chest, the strength of his arms, the scent of him, all man with a hint of leather, was more than Kelly could withstand. She melted against him, telling herself she'd only stay there a minute. Surely she deserved a minute of heaven before she faced the rest of her life without him. As she must.

His lips caressed her forehead again in between soothing murmurs, and one hand slid up and down her back, the movement against her silk blouse creating a delightful friction that spurred her to press closer to him.

"James, we shouldn't be together like this," she whispered, afraid if she didn't protest, she'd give in to the delirious response filling her.

"I can't think of anywhere I'd rather be. What we're sharing is too important, too rare, to be put aside," he replied, continuing to touch her, to entice her.

Recognizing how close to the edge she was coming, Kelly raised her head to tell James he couldn't be a part of her life. She truly was determined to tell him. But his mouth slipped from her temple to her lips just as she opened them to speak.

From their initial surprise to an all-encompassing embrace took only a split second. It was as if long-lost lovers, familiar with every nerve ending, had come together in immediate recognition of each other.

Kelly's arms surged around his neck, and he pressed her against him, their bodies touching intimately their entire length. There was no awkwardness or adjustment. They had been made for each other.

Kelly's body hummed with desire, and she welcomed his touch. Her breasts were heavy, her nipples hard against his chest. While her mind had rejected him time and time again, her body had known what it wanted from the first.

And it wasn't about to take no for an answer now.

Neither would her head.

This was her man, at least for tonight. If that was all she could have, she'd deal with that pain tomorrow.

James's heart leapt with joy as his lips met Kelly's and she didn't pull back. The hunger that had been building in him since he'd kissed her two days ago was greater than he'd ever experienced. He'd been afraid Kelly would run from him if she realized how much he wanted to hold her.

Now, as he pulled her against him, she showed no fear, no distaste, only mutual desire that unleashed the wants he'd tried to hold back. The friendship he'd offered had been real. But he felt so much more for this sweet, determined, stubborn redhead.

He had realized that he wanted a future with her, in whatever capacity she would allow. But he liked the role she was offering right now. That of lover.

In the back of his mind, as the rest of him concentrated on Kelly, he finally admitted that even marriage was a possibility with this woman. He wanted the right to protect her, support her and, most importantly, love her. He was willing to do whatever it took to have her in his life.

He'd promised himself he would never offer commitment to another woman. But he had no choice with Kelly. He was committed to her regardless of what happened.

Then he shoved any thoughts aside. She consumed his head as well as his body. Without conscious thought, he laid her down on the sofa and stretched out beside her, his hands caressing her.

Within minutes they were naked, a mutual-assistance effort that yielded quick results, and James discovered that mere sex could never describe loving Kelly. The warm silk of her skin created a friction that set him on fire. He ran his fingers over her body, memorizing every inch. His mouth followed his hands, eager to taste such perfection.

Kelly wasn't a shy lover. She tugged his head from her breasts to her lips for another drugging, dazzling kiss. He welcomed her demands, wanting to share in every way possible. When he pleased her with his caresses, she murmured her pleasure, spurring him to greater heights. She was a generous lover, giving him gift after gift of incredible pleasure.

The final explosion of their love was so mind-blowing, so magnificent that, afterward, he held her against him, his face buried in her glorious hair, hiding the tears that suddenly filled his eyes.

She was his.

KELLY DIDN'T THINK she ever lost consciousness, but the force of her emotions, the intense pleasure of their coming together, had blotted out conscious thought. Such a sense of completeness filled her that she drifted along, content in James's arms. Nothing mattered but the oneness she felt with him, so much greater than she'd thought it could be.

Strong fingers lifted her face from where it was tucked under his chin, and his lips met hers in a gentle kiss, a salute not only to their passion, but also, she believed, to so much more. She pressed against his warmth and ran caressing fingertips down his cheek.

His lips trailed kisses down her neck as he whispered her name.

Her eyes slowly opened and she stared at the oh-so-familiar print that hung on the wall in her office. Her office. Reality flooded her mind, washing away those tenuous dreams trying to take root.

With reality came a few niggling concerns, such as protecting her heart from the pain that would come, coupled with protecting her body from the loss of his touch. She resented their intrusion. The heaven he'd taken her to hadn't allowed such mundane thoughts of pain.

He lay beside her, his arms wrapped around her, her face nestled against his neck. Every breath she breathed carried his scent. His body warmed and caressed her. How could she leave his embrace?

But those painful thoughts kept pushing their way in, refusing to be ignored, until she had to deny her wants and face her needs. She pulled away from him.

"Kel? Are you—" He pushed up with her, his lips searching for hers as his hands stroked her arms.

She turned her head away and his mouth touched her hair. His hand followed, burying itself in the silken strands to hold her head still. "What's wrong, sweetheart?"

Unable to face him, she closed her eyes. "I didn't intend this to happen."

"This?"

There was a question in the single word. Reluctantly, she opened her eyes and faced him. "I'm not blaming you, James. I think we both realize that there's a—a chemical reaction when we get close to each other.''

"A chemical reaction?"

"Yes," she replied firmly, or as firmly as she could, wrapped in his arms without her clothes, fighting the attraction that their lovemaking had only increased. "I know neither of us intended to do anything that would tie us together— Oh, no!"

"What's wrong?"

"What if I— We didn't take any precautions."

His silence forced her gaze back to his blue eyes, seemingly an even darker blue than before.

"Would that be so awful?"

Kelly sent a prayer heavenward that she wouldn't reveal why it would be awful if he were the father of her child. So awful and so wonderful at the same time. Her child would have the best of fathers. And she would have the worst of heartaches.

How ironic that their positions were now reversed. He wanted to assist in her pregnancy and she wanted— no, *had* to have—the anonymity of the clinic. It made her want to cry.

"Have you already visited the clinic?" he asked, breaking into her morose thoughts.

"Yes."

When he said nothing more, she looked at him again. There was an unhappiness on his face that hurt her without her even knowing why. "I was supposed to go next month for the—the procedure."

"Then you haven't yet—" He broke off his sentence and pulled her against him for a hug.

Startled, and afraid she might lose control again, she pushed away from him. "James, what—"

"Maybe it won't be necessary."

"What won't be necessary?"

"Another trip to the clinic. Maybe you'll already be pregnant."

"James, we agreed that it would be best if—"

"No, *we* didn't agree. You insisted that you preferred using the clinic."

She said nothing. What he said was true, but she didn't want to discuss her decision again. Especially not now.

Feeling awkward, and suddenly aware of her nakedness, she sat up, trying to cover her breasts. "I—I need to get dressed."

"Are you sure?" he asked, his voice filled with the wicked teasing that tempted her more than he knew. "We could try again, make sure we got it right."

"James!" she exclaimed, her cheeks flushed. Probably her whole body was, too, if she dared look. "I don't think there's any doubt that we—we got it right. Would you get up, please?"

Maybe he heard her distress, or maybe he was as ready for this scene to end as she was. Whatever the reason, she let out a sigh of relief as he got up from the sofa.

Before she could stand, he had gathered up her clothing, strewn about the floor, and presented them to her, seemingly unconscious of his own nudity.

"Thank you," she muttered and then watched as he picked up his own. She refused to look away when it might be her last time to share such intimacy.

When his gaze returned to her, however, she switched her attention to her clothes. How was she going to dress in front of him? She could retreat to the women's rest room down the hall, but—

"Need any help?" Again that teasing note in his voice.

"No! No, I'll manage." She stood and turned her back to him, quickly pulling on her underwear and then her skirt and blouse. The panty hose would take too long.

"Kelly," he said soothingly, his arms coming around her as she buttoned her blouse. "Don't be so upset. Our making love was what you'd planned, wasn't it? If I remember correctly, you extended an invitation that first evening."

Her teeth sank into her bottom lip until she tasted blood. How long ago that dinner seemed. With a gasp, she replied, "Yes, but we'd decided—" No. She couldn't say that because he'd only remind her that he hadn't agreed to her decision.

"You're right," she began again. "What happened isn't anything to get upset about." With hard-won determination, she turned in his arms, putting her hands against his chest, only to find it still bare, his shirt unbuttoned. At least he'd already put on his pants.

When he lowered his head, intent on kissing her, she backed out of his arms.

With a bright smile that she hoped didn't look as plastic as it felt, she said, "These things happen. We'll just forget all about it."

He frowned at her, and she prayed he wouldn't ask anything more of her. Her control was fragile, at best.

"Kelly, I—"

"I really have to go, James. I promised Gran I wouldn't be too late this evening." She pulled from his grasp again and rounded the desk to shrug into her jacket, pick up her purse and force her feet into her pumps.

When she met his gaze again, the warm tenderness that had filled it earlier was gone. "I just have one question, since you're in such a hurry," he asked.

"Yes?"

"How long before you know if you're pregnant?"

Chapter Twelve

Kelly stared at him, her heart breaking. She knew he wasn't interested in marriage, or in her. He was only interested in her baby. But somewhere deep in her heart, she must have been hoping she was wrong.

Now she knew she wasn't.

"I'm not sure." She slipped her shoulder bag strap over her shoulder and started toward the door.

He caught her arm, pulling her to a stop. "Do you intend to let me know if I'm a father-to-be?"

One glance at his face, his lips pressed tightly together, his gaze hard, and she looked away. "Of course. Though I'm sure we didn't— Nothing happened."

"You're wrong, Kelly. Something happened, whether it results in a baby or not."

"I need to go, James," she pleaded, her voice scarcely above a whisper.

He finally released her arm and followed her to the door. "Just a minute," he said, and strode to the sofa.

When he reached Kelly's side again, he held out her panty hose. "You forgot these."

She hadn't blushed so much in years. Snatching the panty hose from him, she shoved them into her bag. "Now can we go?"

"After you, Miss Abbott," he replied, but there was no teasing in his voice.

She locked the outer office door while he punched the button for the elevator. Could she pretend she forgot something so she could take a different elevator? James would only wait for her, she thought. If nothing else, he was a gentleman.

He'd only revealed his interest in the child after she'd made it clear she didn't expect any emotion with their lovemaking. How foolishly naive of her to hope for his love, even if their lovemaking had been more than she had even imagined.

She shivered as she thought of his hands on her, caressing, stroking, touching. Under her downcast lashes, she stared at his hands.

"Kelly—" James began, but she was grateful the elevator door slid open.

She walked briskly into the small chamber, made even smaller when James joined her. She jabbed the button for the first floor several times.

"That won't make it go any faster," James observed.

"That's all right. We have fast elevators. I'll have to sign out with Jake, so you won't need to wait on me. I'm sure you have a lot of things to do. It was quite a surprise to discover Ceci is your cousin. I didn't know you had any family here in Dallas. Your mother and dad have retired to the coast, haven't they? I think I remember you saying something about that."

"Arizona," he said solemnly, when she took a breath.

He knows I'm rattling so he won't have an opportunity to speak, but I don't care. I can't bear any more conversation about what happened.

The elevator door opened and Kelly rushed through it. She was out of small talk.

"Jake! How is everything?" she asked with a big smile, as if she hadn't seen him in years.

"Just fine, Kelly. Mr. Townsend's with you, I see."

"Oh, he's leaving. Yes, his car is parked right over there. I'll just go this way since I'm parked in the company garage. Good night, James. Thanks for—for stopping by with those new ideas."

She turned toward the side door that led to the company parking garage only to discover James was still beside her.

"James, your car is in the other direction."

"It's dark. I'll see you to your car."

"That's not necessary. It's perfectly safe. I'll be just fine."

"Kelly," he said softly, his hand closing around the back of her neck, "shut up."

He sounded fed up with her, and she didn't attempt to say anything else. She walked a little faster, however. When she reached her car, she already had her keys out. James startled her by taking them out of her hand.

"James! I can—"

"I know you can. You're an extremely capable woman, Kelly." Without another word, he caught her by surprise again, his lips covering hers.

Instantly, passion flared between them. Kelly couldn't push away, or make any attempt to protest his behavior. She could only return his caress as if her life depended on it. At the moment, she felt it did.

When he pulled away, they were both breathing heavily. She stared at him, wondering why he'd kissed her, but there was no clue in his gaze. Fighting to hold back a sob, she took her keys from him and opened her car door.

After sliding in, she reached to pull the door shut, but James held it open. "Kelly, let me know."

She gave an abrupt nod and pulled the door from his grasp. Of course, the baby. He must have been staking his claim to the child they might have created.

While she was volunteering her entire being for his touch.

The tears rolled down her cheeks, and she never noticed the screeching of her tires as she hurried home.

JAMES STARED AFTER HER disappearing car, his hands on his hips, a scowl on his face. He was confused.

The man was always accused of treating sex lightly, running out on the woman, never calling her again. He had the distinct feeling he and Kelly had reversed the traditional roles.

He was the one left behind, wondering if she'd call. Wondering why what had been an incredible event to him, a special time, had been dismissed by Kelly.

Had it meant nothing to her? Then why the trembling? Why did she refuse to look at him? Why the embarrassment? He couldn't believe it had meant nothing to her. Not when they had gone up in flames as soon as they touched.

So why had she answered the way she did? Why try to act as if their lovemaking had meant nothing?

With a sigh, he started toward his car. He didn't have any answers. He only knew that Kelly was too important to him to give up. He'd wait for her to call. If she did.

She had to.

THEY SAID ALL ROADS led to Rome. But for James Townsend, all thoughts led to Kelly Abbott. Usually, Saturday mornings were for lazing around the house or playing racquetball. On this one, though, he'd woken up early and paced the floor, debating his options.

The problem was, he wasn't sure he had any. By ten o'clock, he was driving himself crazy.

When the phone rang, he leapt for it, sure Kelly was calling.

"Hello?"

"James, did I interrupt something important?"

He immediately recognized an old friend's voice. "Oh, hi, Larry. No, nothing. I was just, uh, thinking."

"Well, I'm calling about our bet. You haven't forgotten I owe you a dinner, have you? Libby and I wondered when you'd like to collect."

Even back in college he and Larry Anderson had been known to take sides with a friendly wager. This time they'd bet on the outcome of a business deal—and James had won.

"No, I haven't forgotten. Whenever it's convenient for you and Libby." Already his mind was wandering back to Kelly.

"I know it's short notice, but how about tonight? Libby and I are free, and we've got a sitter, which is a rarity."

"Yeah, great. Tonight would be fine."

"Who are you bringing along? Libby says if it's that blonde from last time, she won't come," Larry added with a laugh.

"No, not her." James couldn't even remember her name. He hesitated and then said, "I'm dating a special woman now. A redhead. Libby will like her."

"Sounds serious, pal. Are you about to give up the single life?"

"I doubt it. You know I'm set in my ways." Those words weren't necessarily true now. He was trying to find a way to explain the change that had come over him, long after he hung up the phone. Then he sat there, staring at it, as if he could will it to ring again.

Unless Kelly had second thoughts since he last saw her, he didn't think she'd go out with him. But he couldn't take anyone else. Kelly was the only woman he wanted with him.

He drew a deep breath and then picked up the receiver again. He might as well find out now.

"Hello?" The voice wasn't Kelly's, and it sounded older.

"Mrs. Abbott?"

"Yes, who's this?"

"James Townsend. Is Kelly there?"

"No, she's not, Mr. Townsend. And she doesn't work on Saturdays, you know."

She didn't sound any happier with him than her granddaughter was.

"No, of course not. I'm not calling about work."

"Oh?"

Damn, he'd have to explain. "No. I've been invited to dinner, and I wanted to know if Kelly would accompany me."

"I don't know, Mr. Townsend. Kelly went to a party last night and—"

"I know, at Ceci's."

"You were there?" There was a multitude of suspicion in her voice.

"Yes, she's my cousin."

"Ceci's your cousin?"

"Yes. When will Kelly be back?"

"In about an hour. She's at the grocery store."

"Would you ask her to call me?" He gave Mrs. Abbott his phone number and then made one last try to sway her to his side. "I hope she'll call. I'd feel awkward going out with a couple by myself. And I promise I'd get her back early if she wants."

But he'd rather take her home with him and keep her all night.

"I'll give her your message."

"MARY, YOU'LL NEVER GUESS who that was on the phone.

Mary was making a salad for their lunch and didn't even look up. "No, I probably won't. Who was it?"

"James Townsend."

That got her attention. "What did he want?"

"He wants Kelly to go out with him tonight. And he was at the party last night. He's Ceci's cousin!"

"Is that good?" Mary was cautious. She didn't want to celebrate if it wasn't.

"I don't know." Elizabeth paced the kitchen, patting her cheek with one finger. "I'm still not sure he's good for Kelly, but he did sound nice. And I don't want her sitting at home worrying about me."

Mary poured two glasses of ice tea and carried them to the kitchen table. Elizabeth absentmindedly sat down and drank her tea.

"I think she should go!" Elizabeth pronounced.

"But she was out last night. I'm not sure she'll leave you alone again," Mary pointed out.

"Hmm. You're right." Elizabeth thought a moment longer. "I know. I have to buy a wedding present for Janet Casey's granddaughter. Can't stand the woman, but I did get an invitation. We'll go shopping this afternoon and I'll tell Kelly I'm so tired, I'm going to bed real early."

"But, Elizabeth, then she'll worry about you."

"For heaven's sake, Mary, if I act like I'm going to stay up, she hovers over me. That's not healthy for her. What else am I going to do?"

Mary could see no alternative.

"All you have to do, when she asks you how I am, is to say that I'll probably go right to sleep. Tell her...uh, tell her I've been sleeping a lot more lately."

"Oh, Elizabeth, I hate to lie to her."

"It's for her own good. I'm still not sure this Mr. Townsend is good for her, but maybe she'll meet someone else while she's out of the house. She sure won't meet anyone exciting in our living room."

"All right. Where are you going?" Mary asked as Elizabeth got up and started to leave the kitchen.

"I'm going to take those new romance novels you bought me up to my room. I want them handy while I'm pretending to be asleep."

ELIZABETH DIDN'T TELL Kelly about the phone call until after the three of them had shopped for a wedding present. Kelly watched with concern as her grandmother chose the gift without any energy or enthusiasm and then insisted they return home at once.

It was only as Elizabeth was pulling herself up the stairs, assisted by Kelly, that she mentioned the phone call.

"Oh, dear, I forgot. My memory isn't what it used to be. That Mr. Townsend called."

She had misgivings about her plan when she felt Kelly's arm go rigid with tension. After a quick glance at her granddaughter, however, Elizabeth decided to continue. "He invited you to dinner this evening. I'm glad you'll have something to do, because I'm just too tired to keep my eyes open."

"He what?"

"He invited you to dinner. He's been asked out by a nice couple and he'd feel awkward going alone."

"Too bad."

Elizabeth raised her eyebrows at such a cavalier dismissal of the invitation. "Dear, your manners!"

"Sorry, Gran, but I'd rather stay here with you."

"But, dear, I can't stay awake. And it's Saturday night. You should be out enjoying yourself."

"Gran, I'm perfectly happy staying here."

"But I'm afraid I led him to believe you'd go. He sounded desperate. You should at least call him. That would be the polite thing to do. I wrote his number down by the phone."

Kelly said nothing. They'd reached Elizabeth's room by now, and she began helping her grandmother undress. Elizabeth wanted to shoo her away, but she couldn't. She had to make her believe she was too tired to stay awake.

Once she was dressed in her nightgown, Kelly helped her slide into bed. She felt under the pillow to see if her flashlight and books were in place to be easily reached, hoping Kelly wouldn't notice them.

"Promise me you'll call him? I feel guilty about leading him on. He probably won't be able to find anyone to accompany him at this late date, and it's all my fault."

"Gran—"

"Please, Kelly? I feel so guilty," she added again with a big sigh. "Go with him. It's my fault for not telling you earlier."

"I'll call him," Kelly finally said as she turned to go.

"Thank you, child. I'm going to fall asleep before you get downstairs. I'm so tired. And so forgetful."

She closed her eyes and kept them closed until she heard the door close. Well, she'd done all she could for Mr. James Townsend. The rest was up to him.

KELLY HAD JUST REACHED the bottom of the stairs when the phone rang. Mary answered it and then held the receiver out to her. "It's for you, Kelly."

"Hello?"

"Why haven't you called me?"

She had no difficulty identifying the voice.

"My grandmother didn't tell me you'd called until just now. I hope I haven't inconvenienced you." She tried to keep her voice steady. Just hearing him sent tremors through her.

"Inconvenienced me? No, but you've almost driven me crazy! Look, I'll pick you up at seven-fifteen. The reservation is at seven-thirty but it's nearby."

"James, I'm not going."

There was a tense silence, and Kelly prepared herself for an explosion.

"Why?" His single word was so soft, she wasn't even sure she heard it.

"I can't."

"Why?"

"James, this is an impossible situation. I can't date you."

"Kelly, that's the stupidest answer I've ever heard."

"I can't. And you know why. Gran mustn't—" she broke off, remembering Mary's presence in the room.

"Kelly, she's not going to believe the Immaculate Conception story. You have to have been seeing someone if he's going to abandon you."

She hadn't thought about that angle of her story. But she didn't want Gran to think badly of James. Such contradictory thoughts kept her silent. Finally she said, "Couldn't you just ask someone else?"

"Kelly, it's almost five now. Besides, I couldn't ask another woman. That wouldn't be honest. I'm involved with you, whether you're willing to admit it or not."

Involved. As soon as she found out she wasn't pregnant, that involvement would end. When there was no chance he could be the father of her child, he'd find another woman. And her heart would break.

"Okay, I'll—I'll go with you to dinner, but that's all. Do you understand?" She hoped he did. She didn't want to be alone with him again, because she couldn't control her response to him. "In fact, why don't I just meet you at the restaurant?"

"No. I'll pick you up."

"But, James—"

"I'll pick you up at seven-fifteen, Kelly. No arguments."

"Fine," she said huffily, hating to give in to him.

"And, Kelly, it would be nice if we could bury the hatchet and not fight in front of my friends."

"My manners are impeccable, Mr. Townsend!"

There was another tense silence.

"Seven-fifteen," he repeated before hanging up the phone without waiting for her to say goodbye.

Kelly hung up the receiver and surreptitiously wiped away the tear that had escaped her eyes. Her manners might be good, but her self-discipline was another matter. Maybe she could get through the evening without him touching her.

Maybe. But if she did, she thought her heart would break again.

Chapter Thirteen

James watched Kelly as she carried on an animated conversation with his friends. He'd known she would like them. But then, Kelly got along with everyone. Except him. She wouldn't even look at him.

His gaze hungrily traced her features, wishing his fingers could touch her as easily. He longed for the intimacy they had shared.

"You look like you'd rather have Kelly for dinner than the steak you ordered."

"What? What do you mean?" James asked, awakened from his thoughts by his friend's whispered comment.

"You know what I mean," Larry replied, a knowing look on his face.

James shrugged, unprepared to admit anything. "I just like to look at her. I don't get to see her often enough."

"How long have you two been dating?"

Dating? Could he call what they'd been doing dating? That sounded much too normal for what they had shared. But he counted back to that first evening when Kelly had invited him to dinner and was surprised to discover how short a time ago it was. "About three weeks."

Larry stared at him before leaning back in his chair and laughing.

"What's so funny?" Libby asked, breaking off her conversation with Kelly.

"Nothing," James hurriedly said. "Just one of those sports jokes that you don't like, Libby."

"I should have known," Libby said to Kelly. "When these two get together, they always talk sports. I'm glad you're here to talk to me."

"Actually, I hate to confess to you, Libby, but I like sports, too." Kelly glanced James's way and then turned back to Libby.

Amazing. He felt he knew Kelly well, but he was constantly discovering something new about her. He started to question her about what sports she liked when he spotted someone entering the restaurant.

"There's George Canfield. Don't look that way, Kelly. I don't want another meal taken over by him." He liked George, but he didn't want to share Kelly with him this evening.

"James!" Kelly protested, though she didn't turn around. "Mr. Canfield is nice."

"I didn't say he wasn't. Besides, he has his own date this evening." He watched over Kelly's shoulder as his father's friend and a charming lady in his own age group followed the maître d' in the opposite direction.

GEORGE CANFIELD BEAMED across the table at his companion. "Guess what. After your interest in James Townsend, I spotted him across the room as we came in. While we're waiting for our dinner, I'll take you over and introduce you."

Elizabeth Abbott paled. "What? They're—he's here?" She inched her menu up to cover her face. "Can they see us?" she whispered.

"I don't think so. Is something wrong?"

Elizabeth swallowed. Henry had always told her she was too honest to be any good at sneaking around. When George had called a few minutes after Kelly left, she'd thought she could accept his invitation without any problem. She hadn't counted on George choosing the same restaurant as James Townsend. "George, we can't go over there."

"Why not? James won't mind. I've told you, he's a nice boy."

"George, he's with my granddaughter, Kelly." She almost used a naughty word as George's face brightened and he raised up in his chair to look for Kelly.

"You're right, Elizabeth. That's wonderful. Your granddaughter is nice. I can't wait to see her again."

"You don't understand, Kelly thinks I'm home in bed. I can't let her see me here." Elizabeth's patience was wearing thin. She only hoped George would co-operate.

The maître d' returned to their table before George could respond. "Monsieur, we've just had a table near the terrace open up. Since you requested one, I would be happy to accommodate you now."

Elizabeth's gasp must have shown George her preference. A window table would put them very near James and Kelly.

"No, thank you, Pierre. We're comfortable here." He smiled at the man and waited for him to leave the table. Then he turned to Elizabeth.

"I think maybe you'd better tell me what's going on here. Is Kelly mistreating you?"

Elizabeth choked on the ice water she was sipping. "Of course not," she sputtered. "My Kelly would never do such a thing."

"Then why does she have to think you're home in bed? I don't understand what's going on."

"I just wouldn't want her to think I'm spying on her, George. You know how independent these young people are today." She tried a flirtatious smile that had always worked on Henry. George smiled back and relaxed a little. Guilty pleasure filled her to discover that she could still turn a man's head.

"But since I chose the restaurant, she won't think that. And it would be unneighborly of us not to speak to them." His smile faded when she vigorously shook her head no.

"No. She mustn't see me."

George gave her a considering look that increased her pulse rate. "You know, Elizabeth, something's beginning to smell like three-day-old fish."

Red tinged her cheeks, but Elizabeth smiled calmly. "What do you mean, George?"

"I'm wondering why you accepted my invitation tonight."

"Because I wanted to," Elizabeth responded valiantly.

"Now that I think about all our conversations, I'm remembering how you always bring the conversation around to James. I think you're just here to pump me for information."

It was the disappointed look on his face, as if she'd let him down, that really got to Elizabeth. "George," she said, reaching across the table to take his hand, "you're right. I first met you so I could find out about James Townsend. But—but that doesn't mean I don't enjoy your company. In fact, since Henry—since my husband died, I haven't met anyone I enjoy more than you."

"Do you mean it, Elizabeth?" He leaned toward her, watching her carefully.

"I do, George."

It surprised Elizabeth to discover she was telling the truth.

George seemed pleased, but he whispered, "Then you'd better hide, 'cause I think Kelly and her friend are heading to the ladies' room over here."

Elizabeth ducked behind her menu.

"I'VE REALLY ENJOYED meeting you, Kelly," Libby said as the two of them walked back to their table.

"Some of James's girlfriends—well, let's just say I don't think he dated them for their personalities."

The jealous surge that shot through her alarmed Kelly. She had no hold on James. In fact, she'd refused every offer he'd made to her. Except one in her office late one night that she couldn't forget.

She avoided James's questioning look when she sat down.

"Why don't we go back to our house and have coffee?" Libby asked. "That way we can save a little money on the baby-sitter and I can introduce you to the most important member of our family."

Both of James's friends had spoken frequently about their son during dinner, and Kelly longed to meet him and ask Libby questions. But not in front of James. She didn't want him watching her, wondering if she was pregnant. Wondering if he would be a father. She wondered, too.

"It's not too late, Kelly. Is that okay with you?" James asked.

She nodded. "I can't stay too late, though. I don't like leaving my grandmother alone too long."

They ended up staying longer than expected, but Kelly found herself relaxed and laughing, enjoying the evening. When Libby brought Jamie, their son—named after James—into the den and let Kelly hold him, she even forgot her earlier concerns.

"He's adorable!" she exclaimed, cuddling him in her arms. Jamie was fascinated with her hair and kept reaching for it. James leaned over to help her control the little boy.

"He's pretty strong," he added.

"Jamie! No!" Libby said, reaching for the toddler.

"Oh, no, he's fine," Kelly protested, resting her chin on his little head. She smiled at Libby. "I don't often get the chance to play with a baby."

"I think you should have one of your own," Libby said with a grin. "You seem to be a natural mother."

Kelly avoided James's eyes. "I hope to, one day."

"We've been telling James he needs to settle down and have a family, too," Larry chimed in. "I know all newlyweds say that to their friends, but Libby and I aren't newlyweds anymore, and we still feel that way. Especially since this little guy joined us."

"You're still not tired of playing Daddy?" James asked. His voice sounded like he was teasing, but Kelly thought she heard an element of seriousness.

"Nope. Never will be. And we want to have a couple more, don't we, honey?"

Libby rolled her eyes at Kelly. "I love it when he uses *we* when he's talking about pregnancy and childbirth. He almost passed out in the delivery room."

Though Larry blushed, he said, "I'm not real good when there's blood involved. But I hung in there, didn't I?"

"Yes, you did, sweetheart," Libby agreed with a big smile. Then she turned to the other two. "And you should have seen his face when they put Jamie in his arms."

"I wouldn't pass up that memory for anything in the world," Larry agreed, staring at his wife, his eyes filled with such love that Kelly wanted to cry.

IN THE CAR, after leaving his friends, James drove silently, unsure what to say. Larry's description of the birth of his son made James believe his decision to have a child with Kelly was the right one. If only she'd cooperate.

"Kelly—" he began, though he wasn't sure still what to say.

"I enjoyed the evening. I like your friends," she said in a rush, as if to forestall anything he might say.

He decided to accept her choice of conversation. At least they were talking.

"They're favorites of my parents, too. When I brought Larry home from college with me, my mother cooked three times as much food as normal. She called Larry her bottomless pit."

"Did you visit his parents?"

"Larry's an orphan. I think that's one of the things that attracted him to Libby at first. She comes from a big family. The first time she took him home with her, he came back in shock."

"I think it would be fun to have a lot of family around."

"Larry did, too, except in two instances."

He didn't continue, teasing her, waiting to see if she'd ask him to tell her.

"Well?" she finally gave in and asked.

"When he wanted to take a shower or steal a kiss from Libby." He grinned, inviting her laughter.

She cooperated with a chuckle. "You can never have too many bathrooms."

"Or too many kisses."

The tension returned as he pulled into her driveway. Turning off the motor, he caught Kelly's arm before she could open the door. "Don't you think everyone needs kisses?"

"James—"

"I'm just asking to kiss you good-night, Kelly. Nothing else."

When she looked into his eyes, she was a goner and she knew it. Without another word, she moved into his embrace, offering her lips. She didn't need to offer twice.

Once again she proved the theory that there was an incredible chemical reaction between the two of them. At least that was the easiest answer. She didn't want to believe that she'd finally found the one man in the entire world whose touch could set her on fire.

When he pulled away, Kelly struggled to swallow the moan that his withdrawal elicited. How he tempted her.

Without a word, he got out of the car and came around to open her door. Still stunned by the power of his kiss, she had to pull herself together to move at all.

"Thank you for dinner, James."

"Larry paid for it. He lost the bet."

"Well—well, thank you for asking me."

"How about tomorrow?"

She had already taken a step toward the door, but his question stopped her. "What?"

"How about tomorrow? Why don't you come over to my apartment? Your grandmother, too."

"No, I don't think that's a good idea. I think it would be best if we didn't see each other until I have some news about—some news."

"Didn't I just prove I could behave like a gentleman?" he asked, taking a step closer to her.

Kelly backed away. She wasn't worried about his behavior so much as she was her own. Not only was she wildly attracted to him, but she also had a constant urge to tell him about the little things in her life.

She would catch herself at work thinking of his reaction, listening for that warm chuckle that always drew a smile from her. No, she needed to keep her distance. "I'll call you, James, in a week or two," she said firmly, ignoring his question.

"You didn't answer my question."

There was that determination again. "Yes, James, you acted like a gentleman. But I still don't think we should see each other."

She turned and walked resolutely up to the door, even though she would have preferred throwing herself in his arms. When his arm came around her to turn the knob, she jumped in surprise.

"You—you scared me! I thought—"

"A gentleman, remember? I always see my dates to the door."

"Yes, well, good night." She only half turned, not letting her gaze go past his chest, but he bent down and brushed her lips with his one more time.

Kelly rushed into the house as if she were being chased by the devil.

Maybe she was.

HE WAS POSSESSED. James was certain that something—or someone, and he knew who—had taken over his mind and body. The only thing that had gotten him through the rest of the weekend was the thought of work on Monday. He'd have to get control of himself then. After all, he had a company to run. Business had been the center of his life for the past five years.

Not anymore.

He awoke each morning wondering how Kelly was feeling. Lunch was spent considering whether she was eating properly. And the rest of the day his mind was occupied with making love to her.

On Wednesday, when Tex called to set an appointment for the advertising presentation James was ready to race to their offices at once.

"Well, now, that's mighty accommodatin' of you, James, but I was kinda hopin' for Friday afternoon, about four o'clock."

"Friday?" He cleared his throat, hoping to disguise the anxiety in his voice. "Sure. I can make it Friday. Four o'clock, you said?"

"Yep. Kelly and her team have some crackerjack ideas. But maybe she's already told you about them."

"No," James replied, sensing the real question. "I haven't seen or talked to Kelly lately." It seemed like years to James.

"Uh-huh. Well, we'll be seein' you Friday, then."

"Right. Thanks for calling, Tex. I'll be looking forward to our meeting. Oh, Tex, Kelly will be at the meeting, won't she?"

"Well, of course. She's the one in charge of your account, remember?"

"Oh, right. It's just that she talked about resigning from the account and I wondered—"

"Nope. She'll be there. And you be on your best behavior."

"I will. Goodbye."

His best behavior? He was always on his best behavior around Kelly. Flipping the calendar pages, he discovered Friday afternoon wasn't quite as free as he'd thought. He picked up the phone and buzzed his secretary.

"Liz, cancel everything Friday afternoon. I have to go over to Bauer, Tate & Warner that afternoon."

"But, Mr. Townsend, you have an appointment with Mr. Smith from the bank. Do you want me to cancel him, also?"

"Yes, Liz. Reschedule at his convenience." He would cancel the president himself to spend some time with Kelly. Now if he could only convince her how important she, and their possible child, would be in his life.

WHEN JAMES ENTERED the offices of Bauer, Tate & Warner Friday afternoon, the receptionist recognized him immediately. "Good afternoon, Mr. Townsend. They're waiting for you in the conference room. Shall I show you where it is?"

"No, I can find it, thanks." He strode down the short corridor, anxious to see Kelly.

Tex was waiting along with the five-member team. James greeted everyone, keeping his words to Kelly businesslike, but he couldn't help lingering over their handshake.

She met his gaze only briefly and then tugged for his hand to release hers. He had no choice but to comply, but his gaze devoured her, looking for any change in her appearance.

"If you're ready, Mr. Townsend," she said, clearing her throat, "we'll begin the presentation."

It was a reminder that the woman on whom he was focused was more than a beautiful body. Not only were her ideas fantastic, her presentation was professional and concise. He would've liked the campaign even if he wasn't interested in Kelly.

"Well, James?" Tex asked when they'd finished, pride in his voice. "You can't ask for a slicker deal than that, can you?"

"No, Tex, I can't. I'm very pleased. Where do I sign?" He smiled at all the team members. Kelly was the only one who didn't look enthusiastic.

"Come on down to my office. Kelly, as head of the group, do you want to witness the signing?"

James frowned as Kelly only shook her head, concentrating on gathering her materials from the conference table. Clearly, she still intended to avoid him.

He had no choice but to follow Tex from the room.

"I don't mind tellin' you, James, I was a little worried about this here deal," Tex said, leaning back in his chair as James signed the agreement. "Whatever's goin' on between you and Kelly... I don't like mixin' business and pleasure. And I don't want you signin' any contract for any other reason than 'cause it's good for you."

James looked Tex straight in the eye. "That ad campaign is top-notch, Tex, and you know it. I'd be a fool to pass it up."

"I know that. Now how about addressin' the other issue?"

"Are you asking about my relationship with Kelly?"

Tex nodded. "That's right. That gal's more than an employee. She and her family have been my friends for a long time. Now that there's just her and her grandmother, I feel responsible."

"I can promise you anything that happens between Kelly and me will be of her choice. I don't want her unhappy any more than you do."

"Good." Tex extended his hand. "Then I'm happy we're doin' business with you."

"Me, too." James rose and shook his hand. Tex escorted him from his office.

James, however, wasn't ready to leave Bauer, Tate & Warner. There was one more thing he needed to do.

He found the office without any difficulty. The closed door didn't stop him. He opened it and walked in. "Don't you think you've avoided me long enough, Kelly?"

Chapter Fourteen

"Why, George, that sounds like fun. Are you sure you can leave the office?"

Mary listened as Elizabeth talked on the phone. Every time George called—and he called a lot—she could see the change growing in Elizabeth. She only wished her friend would share that with Kelly.

After hanging up the phone, Elizabeth spun around. "George is taking me to the movies."

"So you're going to tell Kelly?"

Elizabeth looked shocked. "Of course not."

"But she'll have to know where you're going. When she gets home, she'll ask." Mary couldn't hide the panic in her voice. She didn't tell lies well, especially to Kelly who was worrying herself sick about her grandmother.

"I'll be home before she gets here. We're going to a matinee. Just tell Kelly I'm sleeping extra long today. Then she won't worry about me because I'm getting more rest."

Humming a song, Elizabeth hurried out of the kitchen, racing up the stairs like a teenager.

Mary sighed with resignation. She'd tell Kelly the nap story, but she didn't think it would please her. Oh, well. At least Elizabeth was improving...and having a good time.

KELLY KNEW HIM well enough now to add stubbornness to his list of personality traits.

"James, there's a difference between avoiding someone and being busy." Kelly held her ground under his intense gaze. "And I've simply been busy." She pretended to read over the papers on her desk.

"I've been able to distract you from work before," he said in a suggestive tone that did not go unnoticed by her. "Come on, let's celebrate the great work you did on my account."

"No, thank you. I have other plans."

"Like hell you do! Who with?"

The explosiveness in his voice told her he was as much on edge as she was. "I don't think that's any of your business."

"Well, I think it is. Who are you dating?"

How could he think she was seeing other men when there was the possibility that she was carrying his child? Her outrage must have shown on her face because he immediately apologized.

"I'm sorry. My temper got the best of me. Look, Kelly, let's not play games. I'm going crazy—"

"I don't know yet if I'm pregnant." There, she just spat it out. She knew that was what he wanted to know anyway.

How she wished she did. Wished the next few days would hurry by so that she could put her life back in order. Since meeting James, she'd lost control of the day-to-day events. And her heart.

"That's not why I'm here, Kelly. I—I just wanted to see you." He paused and drew a deep breath. "I'd just like to be with you."

Her teeth sank into her bottom lip as she tried to hold back the desire to go to him. He appeared as confused as she was. But she mustn't give in. "I'm sorry, James, but I don't think that would help any. We just have to be patient until we find out something. Then you can get on with your life."

He frowned and seemed ready to protest when the phone rang.

"Yes? Oh, I'm sorry. No, that's all right, I understand. I probably should go home to Gran, anyway. Okay, 'bye."

"Your plans got canceled?" James asked as she hung up the phone.

"Yes, but it's just as well."

"What were you going to do?"

"Go to the Dallas Museum of Art. They're opening a new Impressionism exhibit today." She wished he'd leave. Soon he'd discover that she was only going with Linda, and she didn't want him to know that.

"I love Impressionism."

His monotone statement, as if he were reciting an incomprehensible statement, had her looking at him for the first time. "What?"

"Just checking to see if you thought I was an idiot and didn't know what Impressionism was," he assured her with that sideways grin that always got to her. Would their child— No, she wasn't going to think of that.

"So you do know what it is?"

"Of course. My favorite is Monet, but I'd take a Renoir if they were giving it away."

"Generous of you."

"Let me go with you, Kelly," he said, watching her carefully.

"I really should go home. I haven't spent much time with Gran lately, and—"

"Call and check on her. We won't stay long. Just an hour or two."

Knowing she was giving in to temptation but unable to stop herself, she picked up the phone again and called home.

Mary's voice sounded faint, reluctant, when Kelly asked after Gran.

"Uh, she's still sleeping."

Automatically looking at her watch, Kelly saw it was four o'clock. "Still? I thought she only napped after lunch."

"Well, uh, she seemed extra tired today. I thought she'd be, uh, up by now, but she's not."

The doctor had warned her about her grandmother taking less interest in life, sleeping longer hours. But Kelly had been hoping she was improving. Now her heart sank as she listened to Mary.

"Well, Mary, I'm just going to stop at the new art exhibit at the museum for a couple of hours, but I should be home by six or six-thirty, so I can have dinner with the two of you. Okay?"

"Yes, of course, Kelly."

She frowned again. "I'll see you then."

She hung up the phone but before she could speak, James said, "I got the message. We'll make it an early evening."

He was promising to be on his best behavior. As if he thought that would make him easier to resist? She'd finally learned that she had a susceptibility to James Townsend that extended to all his moods, all his behavior, all of him. She only hoped James didn't discover that weakness.

THOUGH THE EXHIBIT was crowded, James felt that he and Kelly were a small island, apart from everyone. He discovered that they had similar tastes in art, too, though Kelly's tastes extended to modern art, also.

He'd never seen much in slashes of red and yellow against a white canvas, unless it was painted by a man in the throes of passion dealing with a stubborn woman. Like Kelly.

She allowed him to take her arm to steer her through the crowds. Once he'd held her hand for about five minutes—until she realized it and drew away.

But at least she talked to him.

One picture intrigued them both. It was the artist's version of a family picnic, nineteenth-century style.

"Doesn't that look idyllic?" Kelly asked.

"It's a beautiful painting, but I don't think I'd want to go on a picnic dressed in a suit," he complained, studying the elegant characters.

"But they look so beautiful."

"Yeah, but even the little boy is in a suit. That's pure torture to a kid." He couldn't help thinking that he'd never treat his son like that. He'd be able to play to his heart's content in jeans, tennis shoes, a T-shirt.

"But they let him bring his dog along. Doesn't that count for something?" she asked with a smile.

"Yeah. Every boy should have a dog."

"Every girl, too. Let's not be sexist."

"Did you?" He studied her as she looked at the painting. Even the masterpiece wasn't as interesting to him.

"Yes." She told him about her childhood pet, and suddenly self-conscious, briskly moved to the next painting.

With one lingering glance at the little boy with the dog, James followed in her footsteps.

A CROWDED MUSEUM was the best place to be with James. There, she didn't have to worry about throwing herself into his arms—or him pulling her into them. They just walked around and talked. And by the time they left, she loved him all the more.

When she got home, there was no time to think about James. Despite having slept all afternoon, Gran seemed so tired. After dinner, she went back upstairs to bed even though it was only eight o'clock.

Kelly wondered if her plan was too late. Would she find out she was pregnant only to discover it was too late to save Gran? She curled up in a ball on her bed, clutching a pillow, fighting the tears that filled her eyes.

She was so emotional lately. Usually she never shed tears but lately— She swallowed suddenly. Did that mean—

No, she wouldn't even think about that. Couldn't think about that. Besides, it was too early to tell.

She simply closed her eyes and forced herself to sleep.

That night she dreamed—about a little boy, his daddy and her. And this time, the daddy had a very handsome face, easily recognizable, at least to her.

KELLY FELT THE STARES. Eyes turned on her, questions in every pair. Questions she didn't want to answer. Beads of perspiration broke out on her forehead, even in the chilled air of the drugstore.

She swiftly turned down a different aisle. Oh, no! The baby food aisle. Spinning around, she breathed deeply in relief when the next aisle contained gardening materials. No one cared who bought weed killer.

Then the chemical smell assailed her and she coughed. She couldn't win.

Beauty aids filled the next aisle and she was able to relax slightly. She studied mascaras intently, as if about to make a life-or-death choice. When her breathing steadied and her heartbeat returned to its normal pace, she looked back down the center aisle cutting across the store.

Three aisles away. That's how far she had to go. Carefully, she checked for acquaintances. There couldn't be anyone here she knew. In spite of her need to hurry so she wouldn't be late to work this morning, she'd driven ten miles away from her neighborhood and chosen a huge drugstore, known for its vast quantities and bargain prices.

Just to buy a pregnancy test.

She hadn't realized how conservative she was. Her Pilgrim forebears must be turning over in their graves. *I'm a wimp!* With a sigh, she threw back her shoulders and attempted a casual stroll across the store.

Turning sharply, she approached the area with the pregnancy tests. Her dismay returned when she discovered them. Eight different brands? Good heavens, how did she choose?

One brand caught her eye. She remembered admiring the advertisement showing a loving couple sharing the moment of truth. Not for her. She would face that moment alone. She looked for another brand.

Ah. There was one that advertised its simplicity. That's what she needed. After all, she'd almost flunked chemistry in college. With a sigh of relief, she reached for it and her eyes fell to the shelf below.

Jerking her hand down, she stared in disbelief. Condoms on the next shelf? Rows and rows of condoms. Couldn't they have put them in separate places? Okay, so she wasn't a modern woman. She'd never bought a condom.

With a shudder, she blindly grabbed the pregnancy test and shoved it in the small basket she carried as she rushed down the aisle. Headache medication joined the test in the basket, as well as a box of tissues, paper towels and, because it was on the next aisle, a small bag of dog food. It filled her basket and covered the pregnancy test.

She chose the checkout stand with the female checker who, fortunately, had the shortest line.

"Mornin', dearie. You find everything you need?" the woman asked, chewing on a piece of gum.

"Uh, yes, thank you." Kelly pulled out her billfold and carefully searched for her money, taking as long as possible to avoid looking at anyone.

"What kind of dog you got?" the checker asked.

"What?"

"Dog. You know, a beagle, shepherd—what kind?"

"Uh, a Lhasa," Kelly muttered, automatically thinking of her childhood pet.

"Oh, honey, you've got the wrong food for a Lhasa. We've got one of those little dickens at home, ourselves. You need to get a different brand. The one in the yellow sack."

Kelly stared at her blankly.

"Here, honey, I'll take care of it for you. Billy, over here."

"Oh, no, no, that's all right."

"Gosh, it's no trouble. Billy, take this back and bring me a small bag of that yellow dog food."

Kelly stood there in agony, fighting the urge to grab the package containing the pregnancy test and run out the door. But then she'd be arrested for shoplifting. Still, it was a temptation, except that they'd list what she'd stolen on the police report and probably publish it in the newspaper!

"Here you go, dearie," the checker assured her with a beaming smile. "This is what you need. And see, I even saved you twenty-one cents."

"Th-thank you," Kelly muttered as she paid the bill. She stood frozen while Billy, the package boy, bagged her purchases and then offered to carry them for her.

"No, I'll manage, thank you." With a fleeting smile, she took her bag and ran from the store.

Once she got behind the wheel of her car, she bowed her head and breathed deep gulps of air. How she hoped she never had to do such a thing again.

Chapter Fifteen

Work was impossible. James shoved his chair back from the desk and rose to pace the room again. He'd been watching the phone all morning, waiting for Kelly to call, even though he had no reason to think she would. It had been more than a week since he'd gone with her to the museum.

Suddenly it struck him that he didn't have to rely on Kelly to tell him when a pregnancy test could be used.

He reached for the phone and dialed the pharmacy he frequented. The pharmacist gave him the information he wanted right away. Grabbing his suit coat, he pulled it on as he hurried past his secretary.

"I don't know when I'll be back, Liz. Let Peter deal with whatever comes up."

"But, Mr. Townsend—"

He ignored her protest and hurried for the elevator. There was more to life than work.

The nearest drugstore catered to office workers. James wandered up and down until he found the aisle he wanted. He was astounded to discover how many choices he had in pregnancy tests. Frowning, he picked up one and then another, reading the packaging carefully.

When a young lady stopped her shopping cart beside his, he looked at her with a puzzled smile. "I didn't know there'd be so many of them."

"I know. The first time I tried one, I was at a loss."

"You've tried some of these?"

"Yeah. A couple of times. My husband and I are anxious to have a baby. We didn't want to wait until a doctor would see me."

She, too, was looking at the tests.

"And did you have a baby?"

Her smile held a touch of heartbreak as she said, "Not yet, but we haven't given up hoping."

"If you'll tell me which one to buy, I'll pay for yours, too," he offered impulsively, "and maybe we'll both be lucky."

"Oh, you don't have to do that. This test is the one I like. You know, they show it on television, with the couple talking about how much they want a baby."

James thought he saw tears in her eyes, so he reached up for two of the tests she'd just indicated. "Come on, let's go buy our tests. I bet we both get good results this time."

He stopped by the gift-wrapping aisle and picked up a card and wrapping paper and a bow.

"Wow, I've never heard of anyone gift wrapping a pregnancy test before," his new friend exclaimed.

He grinned. "Me, neither, but I want to surprise her."

At the door of the store, he wished the lady good luck, hoping, though he'd never see her again, that her wishes were granted. And his own.

Somehow, he didn't think it would be a good idea to present Kelly with his gift in person. After writing a brief message on the card for her to call him, he took the newly wrapped gift to a messenger service and paid a ridiculous amount to have it delivered.

"HEY, KELLY, is it your birthday?" Linda asked, strolling into her office.

A thousand miles away, thinking about the possibility she was facing, Kelly almost fell off her stool behind her drafting table. "My birthday? No. Why would you think that?"

Linda pulled her hand from behind her back and offered what it was holding to Kelly. "This was just delivered to you. I signed for it since I was at the reception desk. I hope that's all right?"

Kelly eyed the package as one might the lit fuse of a stick of dynamite. Why would someone send her a gift? Foreboding filled her. It had to be James. His other gift had been a pregnancy manual. What if this one— She quickly looked at Linda.

"Uh, thanks, Linda." She took the package and set it on the floor behind her desk before turning back to what she was supposed to be working on.

"Aren't you going to open it?"

"No, thanks. It's just—I ordered some—some cosmetics from a new company and they gift wrap their deliveries."

"Cosmetics? Can I see? I've been wanting to try something new."

Kelly almost groaned. She should've known. "Sorry, but I'm on a tight deadline, Linda, and Tex will be a bear if I don't finish up. Maybe tomorrow."

"Okay, but don't forget to give me the name of the company so I can order from them," Linda reminded her as she left the office.

Kelly followed her to the door before closing it. She'd feel better if it had a lock. With a straightening of her shoulders, as if facing a firing squad, she picked up the package.

After opening the card and reading James's message about calling him soon, she set the card down and slowly unwrapped the package. As the loving couple on the box—the same she'd stared at only this morning—appeared, Kelly ground her teeth together.

A pregnancy test!

He'd dared to send her a pregnancy test! And he chose the one she rejected! Without thought, she hurled the box into her trash can.

Sanity returned a moment later, and with it the realization that she couldn't leave a pregnancy test in her trash can. The janitors might start all kinds of rumors! And she supposed she could give James the benefit of the doubt. He was probably only trying to be helpful.

What did she do with the stupid test now? The one she bought was safely hidden in the car. Opening her purse, she tried to wedge it inside, but it was too big. Frustrated, she stared at it as if it really were a bomb.

Finally, she found a sack from a purchase she'd made, and tucked the package and its wrapping inside. At least she could get it out of the office without anyone knowing about it. Then she'd find some unsuspecting trash bin and make a deposit.

And when she talked to James Townsend, she'd tell him that next time he should send flowers.

"HI, GRAN. I'm home," Kelly called as she entered the back door that afternoon. She sighed; it had been such a stressful day. And tomorrow wasn't going to be any better, she told herself. That was when she took the test.

"Hello, dear," Gran responded, smiling at her. "What are you doing home so early?"

"I heard Mary was making green enchiladas. I didn't want to miss them."

"Well, I'm not very hungry," Gran said faintly, shaking her head. "I think I'll just go on up to bed. Of course, that means a lot of food will go to waste. Oh! I should've thought of that before. You can ask that nice Mr. Townsend to join you for dinner. Mary could serve you in the dining room. She won't mind eating in the kitchen."

Kelly stiffened in shock at her grandmother's unexpected suggestion. "I don't feel up to company tonight, Gran. Besides, I don't think Tex would want me to entertain a client here alone."

"Oh, dear, then I hope I haven't done anything wrong."

Beginning to feel that she'd walked into the middle of a film, Kelly stared at her grandmother. "What are you talking about?"

"Mr. Townsend called, and when I told him you weren't home yet, he asked if he could bring over a present for you. Well, I couldn't say no, after he'd gone to so much trouble."

Kelly's thoughts were spinning and she sank down into a chair at the kitchen table. Another "gift"? She'd kill him! Just wait until he got here!

"Dear, are you all right? You seem pale all of a sudden," Elizabeth asked in concern.

The doorbell stopped Elizabeth and brought a wave of nausea to Kelly's stomach. She hadn't had much appetite lately, but she hadn't felt light-headed before.

"Kelly, answer me. Mary, quick, get her some water."

The doorbell rang again.

Mary gave her a glass of water and stood anxiously over her as she sipped it. Elizabeth patted her hand as she sat beside her.

When the doorbell rang a third time, Elizabeth sent Mary to answer it. "Dear, I hope I didn't do anything wrong."

"No, of course not, Gran. Mr. Townsend shouldn't have bothered you here at home. I'll explain to him that he must make calls only to the office."

"But you're so pale."

"I'm just tired. It was a long day."

"Well, if everything's all right, I'm going on up to bed. You have a nice dinner with Mr. Townsend."

Mary came back into the kitchen, and Kelly asked her to assist Elizabeth up the stairs to bed.

"But, Kelly, Mary is going to serve your dinner."

"Don't be ridiculous, Gran. If James stays for dinner, we can serve ourselves, and Mary can join us. The Civil War ended years ago. We don't have servants. Only friends," she added, smiling at Mary.

"In that case, I might just stay upstairs and read to Elizabeth. She likes me to read to her before she goes to sleep, and I'm not very hungry, either." Mary nodded before she and Elizabeth turned toward the stairs. Just before they were out of sight, Mary leaned back toward her. "Mr. Townsend is waiting in the living room."

Let him, Kelly said to herself. The thought of another of his gifts made her want to throw up. Drawing a deep breath to calm herself, and hopefully settle her stomach, she rose and walked to the living room door.

He was standing in the middle of the room, a smile on his face and a big box with a bright red ribbon in his hands. She resented his calm, happy look. Why couldn't he be a nervous wreck, like her?

At least the size of the present told her it wasn't a pregnancy test. Unless he'd bought a year's supply!

"What is it, James? Gran said you called, but I'd rather you—"

"I know. You'd rather I didn't call." His smile dimmed a little. "I have a present for you."

"Another one?" She couldn't keep the sarcasm from her voice.

He gave her a rueful grin that she tried hard to resist. "I gather you got my present today and didn't appreciate it."

"It was totally unnecessary."

"But, Kelly, I thought—"

"I'm not an idiot, James. I can take care of my business without your help."

He sighed. "I'm sorry. I was just trying to be helpful." He extended his arms with the big box. "Will you take this off my hands, please?"

"You shouldn't have bought me a another present. There's no reason." She didn't want gifts from him, she reminded herself, trying to keep her anger. But it was hard. She'd always been a sucker for surprises.

"Come here, Kelly," he said insistently, his voice a husky temptation. It reminded her of the tone he'd used as he'd held her in his arms and made glorious love to her.

As if mesmerized, she moved toward him, only to come to a dead stop. The late afternoon sun sent a shaft of light across his pin-striped suit, highlighting a blond hair on his breast pocket.

She had no claim to James Townsend. She knew that. But she'd rather not know it quite so well. She abruptly turned away.

"What's the matter now?" James asked. When she didn't respond, she heard his footsteps as he moved to her side.

"If you don't want the present, I'll take it away, but at least look at it," he said softly.

She spun around to face him. "I love presents," she said with false gaiety, "but I hate to keep you from other social engagements." With that fake smile pasted in place, she reached out and plucked the blond hair from his suit. "I wouldn't want to disrupt your social life with whomever this belongs to."

He stared at her, a dumbfounded expression on his face before suddenly breaking into chuckles. When she didn't join him in his amusement, he nudged her with the box. "Just open your present. Then I'll introduce you to my blonde."

"She's here? You brought her here?" She couldn't control her outrage, though she tried to bring it under control.

"The box, Kelly."

The dratted man was insistent. She wasn't going to keep his present, no matter what it was. And he could just take his blonde and get out of her house.

While her thoughts were burning in her head, her fingers seized the lid and stripped it from the box. The bundle of fur that was shivering with fear inside yipped at her. She couldn't believe her eyes.

"A dog?" she gasped, immediate tears filling her eyes. "You bought me a dog?"

"A Lhasa. Is it all right?"

With tears spilling down her cheeks, Kelly lifted the trembling puppy from its box and cuddled it against her.

"I—I can't thank you enough, James. It's the sweetest thing I've ever—"

"Are you sure? A minute ago, I thought you'd throw the blonde back in my face."

James watched as comprehension dawned on Kelly. Through her tears, a smile formed on her soft lips. "This is the blonde that left a hair on your coat?"

"Of course. My taste runs to redheads, Kelly, not blondes." Taste? More like an overwhelming passion. He settled her and the dog against him, taking advantage of her emotional reaction.

A little pink tongue darted out from the mop of fur and licked Kelly's cheek. While she was distracted, he wiped away the tears with his thumb.

"Happy with your present?" he couldn't resist asking.

"Oh, James, it's the best gift I've ever received. How did you know?"

"I didn't. But that painting we saw got me to thinking. And I thought I'd better follow up my other present with something better. I remember my dog. He was my best friend for a while—until I discovered girls."

She smiled at him, and he decided the dog had more than earned its keep. To have made her happy, to have wiped away the worry and unhappiness, was worth any price.

"Will your grandmother mind?" he asked again.

"I don't think so. In fact, it might be very good for her. She can take care of— What's her name? Is it a her?" Kelly suddenly asked.

"Yes, it's a her. And she has no name. You get to name her." He continued to caress her cheek with his thumb, enjoying holding her in his arms. When she realized where she was, he knew she'd pull away. But for a few minutes, he was delighting in their closeness.

"I get to name her? Do you have any ideas?"

His body was full of ideas, but he drew a blank on names. "No, I'm all out of names. You got any?"

"We could name her Blondie," Kelly suggested, a roguish look in her eyes. "It would be a constant reminder not to leap to conclusions."

She was too hard to resist. He leaned down and kissed her, a passionate caress that only increased the desire that filled him. When he finally raised his head, the puppy was yapping at them and they were both out of breath.

Unfortunately, Kelly realized she was still in his arms. She backed away, her gaze on the puppy. "I'd better get Blondie some water," she gasped. Spinning around, she rushed from the room.

James took deep breaths and paced back and forth, trying to gain control. He was calm and collected until Kelly returned. Then his temperature shot up again.

"She wasn't thirsty," she said and then, after hesitating, said, "By accident, I have some dog food for her, so I'll feed her in a little while."

His brow rose in surprise, but he didn't ask any questions. Something in her attitude told him not to. "I bought some dog food and accessories essential to the well behaved Lhasa in the bag by the door, too. There's even a book on how to train her."

Kelly rolled her eyes. "You like to buy books, don't you?" she teased, delighting him.

"Yeah. Did you ever read the other one?"

Her face sobered at once, and James regretted his question.

"No, I haven't. I figured there was plenty of time."

His stupid question had spoiled her happiness. He backed toward the door. The best thing to do now was leave and let her enjoy her gift. Even if that wasn't what he wanted to do.

"I'll see you, uh, talk to you tomorrow," he said casually, then added as she looked upset again, "or, uh, sometime soon."

He couldn't resist a quick step forward and a brief kiss. Then he hurried from the house. To wait for tomorrow, or whenever she called.

Chapter Sixteen

Kelly hadn't expected to get a lot of sleep that night. She was right. But the cause wasn't only her nerves. It was also a small bundle of fur, a puppy who was frightened.

James's gift had entertained all three women in the household that evening. Both Gran and Mary had been excited about the puppy when she'd shown it to them after James left.

Cuddling Blondie against her, she crept down the stairs. Maybe the puppy would like a little warm milk. That was supposed to work on babies. Why not puppies?

While she waited for the milk to warm, she walked around the kitchen, petting the little animal. "I think you and I are going to be best friends, Blondie. I've missed having a pet, even if I didn't realize it."

"I think you're right," Gran said, standing in the doorway of the kitchen.

"Gran! Did I wake you?"

"Not really. I figured that little thing wouldn't let you get a complete night's rest." She walked to Kelly's side and stroked the puppy's head.

The microwave dinged at that moment, and Kelly handed the puppy to her grandmother. "Will you hold her while I pour the milk into her dish?"

She watched surreptitiously as her grandmother cuddled the animal against her. James's gift was an inspiration.

"This reminds me of when your mother was just a baby. Henry and I spent many a night fixing bottles and walking the floor with her. She was such a colicky baby, you know."

"Was it worth it?" Kelly asked, smiling softly at her grandmother's memories.

"Oh, yes. Your mother was a delight. You, too, of course, but we didn't get to walk the floors at night with you. At least, not until you started dating," Elizabeth added with a wry grin.

Kelly set the dog dish on the floor and took the puppy from Gran's arms. As soon as Blondie scented the warm milk, she began wiggling with every inch of her little body.

"You'd think she was starving," Kelly said with a chuckle. She'd fed the puppy before going to bed and now, only four hours later, she was eating again.

"That's the way babies are. When you—if you have a child one day, you'll find out that you have to put your life on hold and arrange everything to the baby's schedule. At least for a while. But you'll enjoy it." Elizabeth smiled at Kelly, reaching out to put her arm around her. "Henry and I hoped you'd have a lot of children, dear, to carry on the next generation, of course. But also because you have so much to give a child."

"I'm not over the hill, yet, Gran," she assured her grandmother, returning her hug.

"Of course not, but you spend all your time worrying about me. You need to meet more interesting men." Kelly said nothing and Elizabeth added, "Though Mr. Townsend seems to be an interesting man."

Kelly thought of the gifts she'd received from James. Yes, he was interesting, at the very least, and he'd be the perfect father. The pregnancy test upstairs waiting for her filled her head.

Moisture on her ankle drew her attention to Blondie, licking her to get her attention. "All finished?" she asked, bending down to pick up the puppy.

"Kelly, you do want to have children, don't you?" Elizabeth asked.

"Of course, Gran. I'd love to have a baby. But I'll need you around to show me how to take care of it," she added with a teasing grin.

Elizabeth's eyes lit up. "Oh, I'd love that. It would be wonderful to have baby in the house again."

That spark of joy she saw in her grandmother's eyes told Kelly she'd made the right choice. No matter what heartache she suffered from her decision, a baby would restore the brightness to Gran's gaze and her interest in living.

Suddenly she was anxious to take the test waiting for her. Anxious to know she was doing the right thing for her grandmother. And herself.

"Time to go back to bed, Gran. Let's hope Blondie thinks so, too." They both started back up the stairs. "You and Mary won't mind looking after her tomorrow while I'm at work, will you?"

"Oh, no, the puppy will be fun. A good substitute until a real baby comes along," Elizabeth added.

KELLY UNWRAPPED the package and read the directions. Then read them again. Maybe it was the lack of sleep that made them incomprehensible. Or maybe nerves.

She rubbed her eyes and tried again. Okay. Not so hard. With the puppy still sleeping on her bed, she went into the bathroom and followed the procedure, though several times she dropped the small cup that came with the home-pregnancy test.

Could she have contaminated the test? She thought about it for a moment and then shook her head. It couldn't be that sensitive. She couldn't be the only nervous woman to use their product.

She felt a moment of sympathy for an old roommate who had been careless and had lived on pins and needles until she'd taken a pregnancy test. At the time, Kelly hadn't thought much about the torment her friend was suffering.

She sent a silent apology to her now.

"Now, I just have to wait ten minutes." That would be the longest ten minutes of her life.

The puppy stirred and Kelly went to the bed. She'd take Blondie downstairs to Gran and Mary while she waited. At least it would give her something to do.

Mary had already arrived and both ladies were in the kitchen. They eagerly greeted Blondie, petting her and making a fuss over her, practically ignoring Kelly until Elizabeth looked up. "Dear, maybe you should call in sick today. I don't think you got enough sleep last night."

"Elizabeth's right, Kelly. You have circles under your eyes," Mary added.

Kelly smiled. That's all she needed, another mother figure to worry over her like Elizabeth. "Thanks, ladies, for making me feel beautiful this morning, but work must go on."

"Now, Kelly, you know you always look beautiful. I just want you to take care of yourself."

Mary's anxious expression, even if she didn't say anything, was just as reproachful as Elizabeth's words.

"I was just teasing you two. I'm going upstairs to— to get ready. Will you take care of the dog?"

Both ladies assured her of their willingness, and she returned to her room. And the results of the test.

Carefully checking the time, she reread the instructions to determine the results. A blue dot. That's what she should look for. If there was a blue dot, she was pregnant.

A blue dot.

She entered the bathroom, her gaze zooming in on the small strip of chemical paper. There, as large as the

moon, as far as Kelly was concerned, was a blue dot.
A huge blue dot.

Her eyes widened with wonder, and sudden panic.

She was pregnant.

THERE HAD BEEN NOTHING to distract James from his
thoughts. He'd tossed and turned all night long, wishing he'd shared his bed with Kelly, just to hold her
against him, feel her warmth, soothe her worries. And
maybe his own.

Sure, he derided himself, *all you want to do is hold
her.*

Well, maybe not all. He'd never felt such strong desire for any woman, even his ex-wife. Or such constant need to see her, hear her, be with her.

He used to tease his parents because they seldom
spent any time apart. His dad rarely even went on
hunting trips if his mother wasn't going. He finally
understood why.

The sun wasn't as bright, the air not as sweet, if Kelly
wasn't beside him.

How was he going to explain his feelings to her when
she only wanted his child? Could he share a child with
her and nothing else?

Even the thought caused a shaft of pain that stunned
him. No. Sometime during the night, he'd come to a
decision. If she was pregnant, they would marry at
once. He'd agree to keep it secret from Mrs. Abbott for
a while. But his child wasn't going to be illegitimate.
Kelly wasn't going to be a single parent. His parents
would have another grandchild to spoil.

The decision had been ridiculously easy to make, after all his protests about marriage. All that had been necessary was a very special woman. Kelly. Whether they remained childless or had a houseful of little ones, he wanted to share his life with her.

With the decision easing his mind for a while, he managed to dress and show up at the office, but he got no work done. Pacing the floor and staring at the phone occupied his morning.

By eleven, he'd finally managed to bury himself in his work enough that he only thought of Kelly every other minute or so. When the phone rang, he reached for it without thought. Kelly's voice changed that in an instant.

"James?"

"Kelly? How are you?" Dumb question. She'd think he was only interested in the results of the test. And he was interested in so much more.

"I need to see you."

He didn't waste time asking questions, except the two essential ones. "When and where?"

"Could you meet me at the park behind Snyder Plaza?" she asked, naming a favorite place in Highland Park.

"Of course. When?"

"Right now? I mean, I can be there in ten minutes."

"I'll be there."

He rushed from the office, his mind in a whirl. It surprised him to realize he hoped she wasn't pregnant. As much as he wanted a child with Kelly, he didn't want her to marry him or have his child for any reason except love. Better to have time to persuade her that their futures lay together.

She was sitting on a park bench in the bright sunshine and he studied her face as he hurried to her side. He couldn't tell anything from her expression.

He moved to her side and gently turned her toward him. "I don't see a smile."

She lifted a confused and troubled gaze to his face. "It's a little overwhelming," she said. Her lips trembled and he couldn't keep from caressing them with his, very softly, very gently.

When he lifted his head, she said, staring up into his eyes, "I'm pregnant."

He wrapped his arms around her, pressing her to him, feeling the warmth he'd wanted so badly all night long.

As he held her, the realization that she was carrying his child seeped through him, filling him with unexpected joy. He'd just decided a few moments ago that he hoped she wasn't pregnant. But he couldn't regret a child.

Her lack of enthusiasm struck him. "Have you changed your mind?" He held his breath for her response.

"No! No, but there are so many things to consider."

He eased her back far enough to watch her expression. "Yes, there are. I thought about a lot of them last night. And I decided I didn't want my child to be illegitimate."

Her cheeks paled and her eyes widened. "What are you saying?"

"I'm saying I want you to marry me." Want. Need. Demand. But Kelly's face wasn't filled with happiness.

"But you don't want to marry. You told me. And—and I told you Gran must think I'm abandoned, alone."

"We won't tell your grandmother, Kelly, but my child is going to bear my name when it's born. My name is going on its birth certificate. This child is mine as well as yours." He didn't understand the sadness that filled her eyes. His hand caressed her cheek. "Okay?"

"I can put your name on the birth certificate without your having to marry me. And no one thinks anything about having a child without marriage these days."

"I do!" he exclaimed, and then tempered his voice as she flinched again. "Humor me in this, Kelly. I'll promise whatever you want, but we need to marry, and at once."

HE'D PROMISE WHATEVER she wanted. Would he promise to love her as much as he already loved their child? Or more? No, he couldn't promise that, Kelly thought sadly, because he hadn't offered her love.

At least he hadn't lied to her, betrayed her, as her fiancé had. And he was promising not to abandon her child as her father had. But she wanted so much more.

She wanted the kind of love her grandparents had shared, the "till death do you part" kind of love. Actually, she already had that kind of love, but it wasn't shared. She knew she would never love another man as she loved James. Whether she had his child or not.

The baby.

In her misery, she'd almost forgotten the precious burden she carried inside her.

She stepped to the phone and dialed her gynecologist's office number. When the receptionist answered, she asked for an appointment.

"Oh, I'm sorry, Miss Abbott, but Dr. Jerrell is booked up for about a month. Is it an emergency?"

Kelly bit her bottom lip. Could her pregnancy be called an emergency? "Not exactly, but I need to see her as soon as possible." In spite of the examination at the clinic, she wanted her own doctor to assure her she would have a healthy pregnancy.

"Well, next month I could— Oh, wait, there was a cancellation called in yesterday. Let me see if it's been filled."

Kelly held her breath.

"No, it hasn't. She can see you at two o'clock next Friday, if you'd like."

"That would be wonderful."

"All right. I've put your name down. Now, I need to know the reason for your appointment."

Kelly stared at the phone, wondering why it was necessary to share the intimate details of her life with a stranger.

"Miss Abbott?"

"Yes. I—I want a complete checkup. And I think I may be pregnant," she added in a rush.

"Fine. I'll make a note of that, and the doctor will see you on Friday."

Hysterical laughter bubbled up in her. The lady would make a note of it. As if it were an everyday occurrence. Probably it was for the receptionist. But not for Kelly.

The phone rang beneath her hand and she jerked away as if it had stung her. After several rings, she gingerly picked it up again.

"Hello?"

"Kelly? It's James. I've made arrangements for next Friday."

She didn't have to ask what arrangements. He'd made it clear before he left that they would be married as soon as possible. "What time, Friday?"

"Ten in the morning. Is that all right with you?"

"Yes, but I made a doctor's appointment for two. It was the only time I could get in before next month."

"Okay. We want to make sure you see the doctor. The book I gave you says you should see the doctor as soon as possible." He cleared his throat and then asked, "Do you want me to go with you?"

Kelly's eyes filled with sudden tears. He might not love her, just the baby, but he was a good man, determined to do his part. How she loved him. "No. Thank you for offering, but I think I'd like to go alone the first time. After—after a while, when they do an ultrasound or something, you can come, if you want."

"Okay. Is there— I want us to go away for the weekend. It won't be much of a honeymoon, but—"

"I don't think a honeymoon is appropriate, James," Kelly protested quickly.

"I think it is. Is there any excuse you can give your grandmother? Visiting a friend? Attending a meeting?"

Why was he doing this? Why torture her with the trappings of a real marriage when all he wanted was their child?

"Kelly?"

"I— There's a college reunion in Austin next weekend. I received the information a couple of weeks ago. I wasn't going to go, but I suppose I could change my mind. Gran wouldn't be suspicious about that."

"Fine. I'll make reservations in Austin."

"Fine." Their conversation was stilted, like two strangers making a business appointment. Not like lovers looking forward to sharing their lives. Tears filled her eyes again. She was going to have to stop imitating a watering pot. It wasn't like her.

"We have to go apply for the marriage license. How about Monday?"

"Can we go during lunch? Since I have to take Friday off, I'd rather not miss too much time."

"All right. I'll pick you up at—"

"I'll meet you. Just tell me where."

"The courthouse!" he snapped. "Shall I pretend I don't know you? We could bump into each other accidentally and make a formal introduction. Or I could have my secretary call your secretary. Or—"

"James, please," she begged and then sniffed, unable to stop herself. "I didn't mean to upset you."

"Oh, Kelly, don't cry, baby. I'm sorry. I guess it's nerves. Getting married makes me nervous."

"You don't have to—"

"Yes, I do, and we are. Don't doubt it for a minute. I'll meet you Monday. And if you don't show up, I'll track you down." His voice softened, caressing her through the wire. "Okay, sweetheart? You'll be there?"

"I'll be there."

And God help her, she would. After all, who could resist a proposal like that?

WHEN KELLY WAS A TEENAGER, she'd dreamed of her wedding day. There had been bridesmaids in pretty dresses, groomsmen handsome in their tuxedos, crowds of guests and flowers everywhere. The center of it all, she had moved about in a flowing white gown, like Cinderella at the ball.

The only thing missing in her dreams had been the groom. He seemed unimportant when compared to the majesty of the wedding.

Reality was a ceremony at city hall.

No guests.

No flowers.

No white gown.

Kelly checked her suitcase one last time before she closed it. The suit she planned to wear during the ceremony hung in a plastic bag on her closet door.

The cream silk was fashioned in severe lines, simple, classic. The only touch of fantasy, to remind Kelly of her childish dreams, was the small hat with a cream netting to cover the top half of her face. It reminded her that she really was a bride.

She bypassed the kitchen when she carried the suit and her bag to the car. James had wanted to pick her up, but she refused again. She'd told Gran that she was going straight from the office to the airport, leaving her car there until her return on Sunday evening.

That was a little bit true.

It had been a busy, unsettling week. Just the knowledge that she was carrying a child affected how she approached even the simplest tasks. That the child was James's made those feelings even stronger.

She'd made peace with herself in the dark hours of the night after he'd insisted on marriage. What was done was done. She was carrying his child, and he wanted that child to have his name.

Even if he didn't love her, he was a good man. A decent man. A man to love. And she did. Whatever happened in the future, her child would have its father's name, its father's love.

With a deep breath, she returned to the kitchen to tell the two ladies goodbye. Mary was preparing Gran's breakfast, and Gran, as had become her habit, sat at the table with Blondie in her lap.

"I have to leave now, Gran. You're sure you'll be all right?"

"Of course I will, dear. I'm glad you decided to change your mind and go to the reunion. You don't get out enough," Elizabeth said, smiling serenely at her.

"You're feeling better, aren't you, Gran?" Kelly had avoided even thinking about that question since she discovered she was pregnant. Had she done all this for nothing?

"Well, I still tire very easily, dear, but with Mary to care for me, you have nothing to worry about."

Kelly vowed to take Gran for another checkup as soon as she returned from Austin. Maybe she'd gone about this the wrong way.

Her thoughts left her unsettled and she hurriedly kissed her grandmother's cheek and then told both ladies goodbye. The urge to confess what was about to occur was growing stronger, and she wanted to leave before she said something she shouldn't.

"Have a good time, dear. Maybe you'll meet a nice young man," Elizabeth called out as she was leaving.

Kelly almost choked. A nice young man. She'd met the nice young man she was destined to love forever. She was going to marry him. She was going to have his child.

And she was going to be miserable because he loved her child but not her.

Chapter Seventeen

Kelly didn't go to the office after leaving home. That would mean answering too many questions. With time to kill, she drove around the familiar streets, feeling foolish. Wandering aimlessly about town on the morning of her wedding was a little strange.

A little after nine, she pulled into a gas station she'd never stopped at before. After filling up her car, she paid for the gas and borrowed the key to the rest room. Closing the rest room door, she looked around the clean but dull and utilitarian decor and sighed.

"What's wrong with this picture?" she asked herself aloud as she looked from the painted concrete floor to her silk suit. "I never thought I'd dress alone in a gas station for my wedding day."

With a fatalistic shrug, she hung the dress hanger on the rest room stall door and began to make the transition from ad executive to blushing bride. When she looked in the cracked mirror over the small sink a few minutes later, an elegant stranger looked back at her.

A stranger who was going to marry the man she loved. And pretend she didn't.

She emerged into the bright Dallas sunshine in her silk cream suit, her hat with its veil in place and pumps to match the outfit.

Just donning the clothes, however, didn't fill her with assurance. When she returned the key to the attendant, his raised eyebrow and appreciative low whistle helped restore her spirits a little.

But she knew, inside, she was still shaky with nerves. She noticed her fingers were trembling when she tried to insert the key into the ignition.

What was she doing? She'd almost married once before. Was she making the same mistake again?

"No," she muttered to herself. She could trust James. He would be honest with her.

Maybe she wasn't having the wedding of her dreams. But the groom was right. She drew a deep breath and settled her nerves. At least that part of her dream was better than she'd ever hoped it to be.

James was the love of her life.

She wouldn't want to marry anyone else, even if they loved *her*. Because James was the one she loved.

Starting the car, she slowly drove in the constant traffic of Dallas to the courthouse. All the while, she kept her mind carefully blank. She'd resolved her doubts. Best not to think of anything else.

James had told her to meet him on the second floor. She pushed the button for the elevator without looking around her. Nothing mattered but reaching James before her confidence eroded.

When she stepped out of the elevator on the second floor, her gaze immediately discovered James, watching for her. She moved toward him in a daze, slowly, with measured steps, as if she were marching down the aisle, the music building to crescendo.

Without saying a word, he convinced her she was beautiful. His gaze lit up, his smile spread across his handsome face, and his lips and arms reached for her. She melted into his embrace, willing, for one moment, to believe that he loved her, too. That their union was a match that would last for all time.

"I was afraid you weren't coming," he whispered after kissing her.

Pressed against him, her face buried against his neck, Kelly whispered, "I promised."

"I know, but—here," he added, pulling back and Kelly looked at him in question.

He thrust into her hands a bouquet of red roses, mixed with baby's breath, and wrapped in silver paper.

"Flowers?" she questioned in a quavery voice. He'd brought her flowers for her wedding.

He kissed her again, briefly, tenderly, and whispered, "For the most beautiful bride in the world."

The flash of a camera startled her.

"Sorry. I hired a photographer, too. I want to be able to share our wedding with my family, and your grandmother when you feel the time is right." He took her arm and turned her toward the offices behind him and waved for the photographer to come after them.

Numbly, she followed his lead.

He quietly notified the clerk that they were ready. Kelly scarcely took in her surroundings. She pressed the roses to her face, loving the scent of them, feeling the velvet texture of the petals against her skin.

His hand tightened on her arm and he led her forward as a gray-haired gentleman entered the room.

"Mr. Townsend?"

"Yes, Your Honor. This is Miss Abbott."

The judge nodded in her direction, a smile on his face, and Kelly nodded in return. She was glad James kept hold of her. If he hadn't, she had the strangest feeling she might have floated away. Nothing seemed real.

"You have the rings?"

Kelly looked at James, sudden panic filling her. Rings? James had asked her ring size, promising to pick up a couple of gold bands, but she hadn't given rings another thought since then.

"Yes, sir," James responded calmly.

"Fine. Then we can begin. Your witnesses?"

Another detail she'd forgotten. James wrapped his arm around her shoulders, as if preparing her for a shock. She looked up at him in time to see him nod to two people sitting in chairs along the back wall.

"My assistant and my secretary are going to be our witnesses, Kelly. It's okay."

A woman in her fifties, a kind smile on her face, stepped up beside her, and a young man took the position on James's right hand. Kelly's gaze flew to James, and he smiled in reassurance, his arm tightening briefly.

The judge began the ceremony, and as he said the words that would unite the two of them as one, husband and wife, Kelly's concern with her surroundings fell away.

She was marrying the love of her life.

That was all that mattered. She was marrying for the right reasons. When it was time to say "I do," she could say it with her head up, a smile on her face, because she loved James with all her heart.

Regardless of *his* reasons.

"YOU MAY KISS the bride," the judge said solemnly.

James didn't hesitate to follow his advice.

He felt as if he'd been waiting for this moment all his life. He'd been waiting for Kelly Abbott to fill the gap, to complete him. Drawing her to him, he kissed her as if he'd never stop. And he might not have if it hadn't been for Peter clearing his throat.

"Uh, James, I think the judge has some more customers."

James lifted his lips from Kelly's, gazed into her green eyes, trying to hide the desire that filled him the minute he got within sight of her, and released her.

"Right. Thanks, Peter, Liz. Peter, take Liz to lunch somewhere nice and put it on the expense account."

With a word of congratulations, his two witnesses left, and he guided Kelly from the room. "You're a beautiful bride, Mrs. Townsend."

"Th-thank you," she murmured, her gaze downcast.

"Do you want to pose for a couple of shots now that you're married?" the photographer asked.

"Yes, of course," James agreed, though photographs weren't at the top of his list. But he'd hired the man to provide pictures of the most important event in his life to date. He might as well let the man do his job.

"Could you smile at your husband, Mrs. Townsend?" the photographer suggested.

"Good idea, Mrs. Townsend," James teased, and tipped her face up toward him with a caressing finger. He slipped his arm around her, pressing her closer. "Now, smile for the picture."

She did so enchantingly, and he kissed her again, unable to resist now that she was his wife.

James lost track of time and the photographer as Kelly responded to his touch. She might not love him, as he loved her, but she wanted him. And God knew he wanted her. Forever.

"Mr. Townsend? Mr. Townsend?" the photographer insistently called.

"Uh, yeah?" James replied, his lips only inches away from Kelly's.

"I'm through with the pictures, unless you want something else. I'll let you know when the proofs are ready."

He nodded and started to kiss Kelly again, but she pulled away.

"I don't think we should—this is a public place," she whispered, her cheeks rosy.

He looked around him, almost in surprise, to discover they were still in the courthouse.

"Right," he agreed, clearing the huskiness from his throat. "I've ordered a meal for us at the Mansion." That was the restaurant they'd dined in when she first discussed her outrageous idea.

"James, we can't go there like this. People might realize what—what we've done," she said.

"We're dining upstairs, in a private room."

"But, James—"

"Kelly, we are going to celebrate our wedding, come hell or high water. I'm not going to have to confess to my child, one day, that I didn't even take his mother out to celebrate our marriage."

He was concerned when the light in Kelly's gaze dimmed a little and she turned away from him. "Kelly? What's wrong?"

"Nothing. I'll meet you there."

"Why don't you leave your car here? I'll bring you back afterward."

"No, that will take too long. I don't want to be late for my doctor's appointment."

He didn't argue with her, but he wanted to. He didn't want to let her out of his sight. He feared she might disappear, and what had just occurred would turn out to be a dream, not reality.

After seeing her to her car, he crossed the parking lot to his own. He'd follow right behind her. She was his, as surely as he was hers. With or without a ceremony, he knew Kelly held him in the palm of her hand. Now, all he had to do was convince her of it. And tonight, he planned to.

KELLY HAD ALMOST REACHED the Mansion, driving automatically, before she noticed the wedding ring on her third finger.

James had assured her, several days before, that he would pick up some bands for them to exchange. He hadn't mentioned that hers would be covered with diamonds. She caught her breath as she examined the beautiful ring.

It must have cost him a fortune. Why had he chosen such an expensive ring when a plain gold band would've done just as well? Did the marriage mean more to him than simply a name for his child? Was *she* more to him than simply the mother of his child?

Oh, God, please, she prayed. *Let him want this marriage to last. Let him want it to be more than a way to have a child.* And finally, she offered her most important prayer, *Let him love me.*

She sobbed as she turned into the parking lot. Was she asking too much? Other women had happiness. Why couldn't she? Perhaps she'd forced the issue with her baby, their baby, she corrected herself. But she loved him. Would that be enough?

Wiping her tears away as the valet opened the door, she stepped out and moved around the car to the entrance. There, she waited for James, who was right behind her.

He gave her another of those brief, sweet kisses that she had come to crave, and took her arm, leading her inside and up the circular stairs.

"Everything's all arranged."

She still carried the bouquet of roses in her hand, unwilling to leave them in the car where they would wilt. She found a matching bouquet on a dinner table draped in white linen in the center of a small room with French doors opening onto a balcony.

"I would have ordered champagne," James explained as they entered the room, "but the book says you shouldn't have alcohol."

Trust James to have read every page. His concern for the child was sweet, but it was also a reminder of the reason for their marriage. In spite of her earlier acceptance, she felt a little hurt that his thoughts were always for the child. "That's all right. I don't mind."

"We're going to toast our marriage with nonalcoholic grape juice instead," he added, a smile on his face. "You'll just have to rely on our emotions to make you high, instead of alcohol."

She blinked to hold back the tears. Yes, her emotions were strong enough to override her common sense. She didn't need champagne.

As soon as they were seated, a waiter appeared with two champagne flutes filled with a golden liquid. James took both of them and handed one to her. The waiter quietly withdrew.

James tapped their glasses together, the sound of fine crystal a chime that she would remember forever, and said, "To our marriage, Kelly. May it—" He stopped midsentence, staring at her, and then said, "May it be fruitful."

With trembling fingers, she drank to his toast.

"JUST BE SEATED, Miss Abbott. The doctor will be with you shortly."

Kelly hoped so. Their flight to Austin left at four. She'd assured James she'd be able to make it to the airport on time.

An hour later, she wasn't so sure.

"I'm sorry, but I have to catch a plane in an hour. Will the doctor be able to see me soon?" she asked the receptionist.

"I was just going to call you. If you'll come back to examining room number two, you can undress and the nurse will be in to administer some tests."

Kelly followed the lady back to the correct room, followed the nurse's directions and finally, when she was lying on the examining table, heard the doctor's voice.

"Hi, there, Kelly. How are you?"

"Fine, Dr. Jerrell."

Louise Jerrell had been her gynecologist since she was a teenager. Gran had found a lady doctor for her to go to, much to Kelly's relief, and she'd liked her at once.

After a brief examination, Dr. Jerrell instructed Kelly to dress and go to her office. Kelly put on her clothes and entered the doctor's office. She opened her mouth to warn the doctor about her flight when the doctor asked her a question.

"Why do you think you're pregnant?"

Everything stopped.

As if in slow motion, Kelly sank into the chair by the doctor's desk. Something was wrong.

"What do you mean?"

"My receptionist said you thought you were pregnant."

"I am. I took a pregnancy test."

"How long after intercourse?"

Kelly told her, but the tension mounting inside her was becoming fierce. "What are you saying, Dr. Jerrell? Aren't I pregnant?"

"No, Kelly, you're not."

"But I must be!" she exclaimed, hysteria rising in her as her gaze fell to the diamond band on her left hand. "I must be pregnant!"

Chapter Eighteen

"Kelly's airplane has probably just taken off," Mary mentioned to Elizabeth as she served her a cup of hot tea to go along with the chicken strips she'd broiled. Elizabeth liked to dip them in hot mustard.

"Yes," Elizabeth said with a frown. "I've been thinking, Mary. Do you think Kelly seemed happy about her plans?"

Mary shrugged her shoulders. "Maybe she was just worrying about leaving you."

"Then you didn't think she was happy!" Elizabeth exclaimed. "I knew it! Why didn't you say something?"

"Elizabeth, I didn't say she was unhappy. Besides, she worries about you a lot."

"She shouldn't be worrying about me. I'm healthier than I've been in months."

"But she doesn't know that, Elizabeth. You've been hiding your gardening, your outings with George. You've gone to bed early and pretended to be weak. I've told her you don't eat any dinner, without mentioning the big snack you have about four o'clock every day. I feel so guilty!"

"Pshaw! It's for her own good. If she knew I was better, she'd never go out. She'd think she has to keep me company. Until you moved in here, she hovered over me."

"With good reason. You know you weren't doing well!"

Guilt filled Elizabeth's face. "I know, I know. That's why I've got to help her be happy. I don't want her wasting her life away worrying over me."

"Well, she's going to spend the weekend visiting old friends. Maybe she'll meet someone nice."

Elizabeth stared into space, unconsciously stroking Blondie as she lay in her lap. "Does it strike you as strange that she suddenly decided to go meet other people when she and James Townsend have been seeing so much of each other?"

Mary shrugged her shoulders again. Before she could answer, however, the phone rang. She reached for it.

"It's for you. It's George," she informed Elizabeth and turned back to her cooking.

George's calls were becoming commonplace to both women. Elizabeth enjoyed their conversations. After more than fifty years with a man in her life, she missed the masculine viewpoint.

"Hi, George."

"Elizabeth, how are you?"

"Fine. And you?"

"A little lonesome. I don't suppose you'd like to accompany me to dinner? You said Kelly was going to be out of town."

Tempted, she looked at Mary, cooking the chicken. She'd had to accept all George's invitations in secret because she didn't want Kelly to know about them. But if Kelly was out of town—

"By the way," George continued as she thought about his offer. "I called James to have lunch with him today, but his secretary said he'd be out of town until Monday."

All thought of dinner disappeared. "Out of town where?" Elizabeth snapped.

"I don't know. She didn't say. Does it matter?"

"Yes, I think it might. Could you find out if he's gone to Austin?"

"Sure. I'll call you right back."

Elizabeth hung up the phone, a frown on her face.

"What is it, Elizabeth?"

"I think I know why Kelly was so unhappy. Do you remember that soap opera we watched where that man seduced all those women?"

Mary nodded.

"Well, I think Kelly is going away for the weekend with James Townsend. He's planning on seducing her!"

Mary hesitated and then said, "Maybe Kelly wants to, you know—lots of young people don't wait for marriage these days."

"Kelly was unhappy!" Elizabeth stubbornly exclaimed.

The phone rang.

"Yes?" Elizabeth snapped.

"He's gone to Austin," George said.

"Then I can't accept your dinner invitation, George. I'm going to Austin."

"But, Elizabeth, why?"

"To protect my granddaughter."

"I won't let you go alone. I'm coming with you. If that boy is doing something he shouldn't, I'll be there to help you."

They made their plans in a matter of minutes, Elizabeth telling him to make a reservation for Mary, too. When she hung up the phone, her companion was staring at her, her mouth open.

"Pack a bag, Mary."

"Why am I going?"

"Because I need you to chaperon George and me."

"WOULD YOU CARE for something to drink?" the stewardess asked in a cheerful voice.

Kelly stared at her, scarcely understanding what she'd said. She was still in shock.

"She'll have a mineral water," James said beside her. "And I'd like the same."

Kelly closed her eyes, ignoring what was going on around her. All she could think about were those few minutes in Dr. Jerrell's office.

Not pregnant.

She twisted the beautiful ring on her left hand. James had married her for the sake of his child. But there was no child. What did she do now?

"Kelly? Here's your drink," James insisted, bumping her shoulder with his since his hands were full.

"What? Oh, thank you." She didn't meet his gaze. She couldn't. It had been impossible to look at him. Fortunately, there'd hardly been time for him to notice since she'd just barely made the flight.

"Kelly, what's wrong? You haven't spoken a word since you got here. Tell me what the doctor said."

She risked one glance at James, seeing the eager anticipation in his gaze, before turning to the window. "Not now, James. I'm very tired."

A puzzled frown was reflected in the window. "Okay. You rest for now. It's a short flight."

She closed her eyes, keeping her face turned toward the window, and remembered again the doctor's words. The pregnancy kits aren't always accurate, especially when they are taken early. It's best to take several to be sure. Tension could have caused all the symptoms she'd thought signified pregnancy. Had she been particularly tense lately?

Hysterical laughter again bubbled up inside her. She'd been about as tense as the owner of the china shop just after the proverbial bull arrived.

What did she do now?

That was the question that she kept hearing over and over again.

But never the answer.

JAMES GAVE THE BELLBOY a tip and closed the door after him with a sigh. All his plans, his dreams, for the weekend were quickly going up in smoke. After pacing the airport lounge, fearing Kelly wouldn't make the flight, he'd been flooded with relief when she showed up.

That relief had quickly turned to puzzlement. She seemed to be in shock. In spite of his questions, she'd refused to explain anything.

He turned to face her now. "How about dinner? They've got a terrific restaurant on the top floor, and I made us reservations for six o'clock." That was a little early for dining, but he had plans for after dinner.

She looked at him wide-eyed, and he wasn't even sure she heard him. "Kelly? Do you want to change for dinner?"

"Yes, yes, I'll change," she agreed, avoiding his gaze.

"Fine. You go first. I'll give you some privacy." His smile didn't quite reach his eyes, but he didn't think she'd notice. Was she frightened of making love? He couldn't believe that was the problem. When they'd made love the one time before, Kelly had been a warm, willing lover.

Just thinking about how willing brought a surge of desire. He wanted her back in his arms tonight, the entire night. He wanted to wake up with her beside him.

But not if she didn't want the same thing.

He rubbed the back of his neck as he paced across the room. He'd be patient. At least he'd try to be patient.

BY THE END OF THEIR MEAL, James's patience was almost at an end. He'd introduced various conversational topics, designed to set Kelly at ease. She'd virtually ignored him. Her meal hadn't interested her, either. She'd picked at the steak cooked to perfection.

Something was wrong, and he was tired of being left out in the cold.

He'd give it one more try.

"How about a dance before we go back to the room?"

Something in his question aroused Kelly. She gave him a wild-eyed look and then abruptly nodded, rising from her chair. He followed her onto the dance floor and wrapped his arms around her.

When she stiffened, trying to move away from him, James held firm. He wasn't about to dance as if they were strangers. Hell, they were married and about to become parents together!

As they swayed to the music, he felt Kelly gradually relax, until she leaned against him, releasing a sigh that shook her. He cuddled her, her body arousing him. He wanted to make love to her all night long.

His lips caressed her neck, down to her shoulder, appreciating the low neckline of her green silk dress, while his hands stroked her back. Her arms were around his neck, and she clung to him, seemingly welcoming his touch.

Finally, when he thought his body could take no more, he led her from the dance floor to their table and handed her purse to her. "Let's go to our room," he whispered, keeping her close to him with an arm around her waist.

She said nothing and he soon had them in the elevator. Even as the car went down, however, he felt her withdrawal. Her body tensed and she pulled away from him.

He wanted to demand an explanation, but he decided it shouldn't come in an elevator. As soon as he opened the door to their room, however, and closed it behind them, he turned to face her.

"Kelly, I've been patient all afternoon. I think it's about time you tell me what's wrong." He walked to her side and put his arms around her, but she pulled away.

"Are you worried about making love? If you're concerned about the baby—"

"No!"

"Good, because the book said it wouldn't affect the baby until the eighth or ninth month," he continued as if she hadn't interrupted. "So we've got lots of time left to—to enjoy each other."

He leaned down to kiss her, but she spun away from him and crossed to the other side of the room.

"Kelly, what's wrong?"

"We can't."

She'd whispered those words and he wasn't sure he'd heard her correctly. "What did you say?"

"We can't."

"We can't what?"

"M-make love."

James crossed the room in a hurry, taking her by the shoulders and turning her to face him. "What are you talking about, Kelly? Why can't we make love?"

She lifted tragic eyes, tears slipping down her cheeks, and opened her lips.

"Because—"

A loud knock on the door startled both of them.

James was torn. He'd like to ignore the knock. They were expecting no one. But if they didn't go away, Kelly wouldn't answer his question. Better to get it over with.

"Wait here," he told her, punctuating his words with a brief kiss that only left him wanting more.

He strode to the door and yanked it open as the knocking increased. Confusion filled him as he faced George Canfield and two older women. One of them looked familiar.... The woman he'd met that first night at Kelly's house. He figured the older woman was Kelly's grandmother. His hunch was quickly confirmed.

"Gran!" Kelly exclaimed, rushing past him to take the oldest woman's hands. "What are you doing here? What's wrong?"

"What are *you* doing here, young lady? Is *this* the reunion?" The woman turned around to glare at James.

James had a few questions of his own. "George, what are you doing here with Mrs. Abbott?"

"Well, James, she said you were bent on seducing her granddaughter, and I couldn't let her come alone."

"Oh, Gran!" Kelly moaned.

With an exasperated sigh, James pulled the door wider. "You might as well come on in. I'd rather not discuss my personal business out in the hallway."

The living room of their suite now seemed much smaller. Rather than taking one of the chairs, James leaned against the wall, watching the lady who'd prompted Kelly's first approach to him.

"I thought you said your grandmother was ill, Kelly?" he asked, puzzled.

"She is," Kelly agreed.

"Of course I'm not," Mrs. Abbott assured him in a strong voice.

"Gran, you know the doctors said—"

"What do they know? I'm just fine, dear."

"But you haven't been eating your dinner. You go to bed before the sun goes down. Isn't that right, Mary?"

The other lady, a few years younger than Mrs. Abbott, backed against the wall near the door and only nodded, avoiding Kelly's gaze.

"I think Mary has more to say," James prodded, having watched guilt fill the other lady's face.

She threw him a startled look and then pushed away from the wall. "Kelly, she is eating properly. She just has a big snack about four after doing the gardening. That's why she doesn't eat her dinner. And—and sometimes, she was out with George when I said she was sleeping."

"Mary, you traitor!" Elizabeth retorted.

"Elizabeth, you know it's true. You've been hiding your good health from Kelly, and it makes me feel so guilty!"

"But I told you it's for her own good."

"Gran, why would you think it would help me to think you're sick?" Kelly moved over to sit on the sofa and take her grandmother's hands in hers.

"I want you to be happy, dear. I didn't want you staying at home worrying over me."

"Oh, Gran," Kelly said with a weary sigh.

"You're such a good child." Elizabeth hugged her. When she sat back, she eyed James with a frown. "Now, young man, what have you got to say for yourself?"

James shrugged his shoulders and offered a smile. "Welcome to the family?"

"James!" Kelly gasped.

"What family? What are you talking about?"

Since her grandmother was well, Kelly had no reason to hide their marriage or the child. James was relieved that the secrecy was over. "My family. If you're going to be my baby's great-grandmother, you're part of my family, too."

All three of their visitors seemed stunned. But Kelly's reaction troubled him the most.

"No, James, please don't," she pleaded in a low tone of voice.

But he'd had enough secrecy.

"Kelly, there's no reason to keep quiet, now."

"Yes, there is. I haven't told you—"

"You seduced my granddaughter?" With outrage in her voice, the petite woman jumped up from the sofa and drew back her arm as if she intended to level the six-foot-plus man before her. George and Mary grabbed her even as Kelly cried out.

"I insist that you marry her at once."

"You don't have to insist. Your granddaughter and I were married this morning. We're now on our honeymoon. Not exactly as I pictured it, I'll confess, since I'd counted on a twosome only, but I'm glad we don't have to keep it a secret any longer."

Elizabeth turned to stare at her granddaughter. "Why did you keep it a secret at all? I've been wanting you to find someone to love, Kelly. I couldn't be happier!"

George moved over to shake James's hand and Mary exclaimed with joy. Only Kelly seemed unhappy about what had occurred.

"Kelly?" Elizabeth prodded when her granddaughter didn't respond. "What's wrong? Aren't you happy to be married to Mr. Townsend? He didn't force you, did he?"

Kelly gave a laugh that sounded hysterical to James. He moved closer.

"No, he didn't force me. I—I forced him!" Kelly exclaimed before covering her face, her shoulders shaking with sobs.

There was a babble of confusion, but James ignored all the questions. He reached down and lifted Kelly to her feet and enfolded her into his arms, pressing her against him, holding her while sobs wracked her body.

"Sweetheart, don't cry. We'll work it out, whatever is wrong," he murmured, but he didn't think she heard him. All he could hope was that his strength and warmth would reach her.

"What have you done to my granddaughter, young man?" Elizabeth demanded, reaching out to pat Kelly's shoulder. "How dare you make her unhappy!"

"I think it's just because of her condition," he muttered, still stroking her back and kissing her forehead.

His words must have reached her because she pulled out of his arms, a stricken look on her face.

SHE COULDN'T LET JAMES tell her grandmother the lie that had been hiding inside her for all these hours. Pulling away from his comfort was difficult, but she had to stop him.

"No, James, it's not my condition. Don't you see? It's not true!"

"What's not true? I don't understand what's going on here," Elizabeth complained. The other two, George and Mary, were looking uneasy, and Kelly realized she must appear deranged to all of them.

But the only one who mattered was James.

"The—the test was wrong, James. I'm not... I'm not." She couldn't bring herself to say that word, but she knew he'd understand.

"Not what?" Elizabeth demanded again.

It was James who supplied the answer, his gaze never leaving Kelly's. She thought she'd die when she read the disappointment in his eyes. It only intensified her own feeling of loss.

"She means she's not pregnant."

"Well, that doesn't matter. You seduced her, so I'm glad you got married. It's only right."

George gave an embarrassed laugh. "You know, Elizabeth, some folks don't always...marriage isn't always...well, you know what I mean."

"Exactly what I said," Mary added with an I-told-you-so nod.

"In fact," George continued, "I think maybe we should go to our rooms and let these two be alone. After all, they did get married and they're on their honeymoon."

Kelly panicked. She couldn't be alone with James. Not when she wanted him so badly. Not when she feared she'd break into more sobs at any moment. Not when she wanted him to love her more than anything in the world.

"Oh!" Elizabeth exclaimed, turning to look at Kelly and James. "I suppose...are you sure this is what you want, Kelly?"

With an effort, she broke her gaze from James's and looked at her grandmother. "It doesn't matter what I want, Gran. Our marriage isn't— There'll be an annulment."

James suddenly spoke. "George, if you'll escort these two ladies to their rooms, I'd appreciate it. There's a wonderful restaurant on the top floor. Take them there for dinner, my treat."

"Kelly, are you coming with us?" Elizabeth asked, a frown on her brow.

"Yes, I'll—"

"No. My wife will be staying here with me."

"But she just said—" Elizabeth began.

"Mrs. Abbott, my wife and I have some things to discuss...alone. If she wants to join you afterward, you have my word I won't stop her."

He wore a stern look on his face, and Kelly didn't blame him for being angry with her. She hadn't tried to trick him into marriage, but the result was the same. She wished...But she owed him an explanation. At least, now, with Gran...well, there was no desperation. If she had a child, it would be for the best reason, because she wanted one. No other reason.

"Is that all right with you, Kelly?" Elizabeth asked, watching her. "You don't have to stay if you don't want to."

"I know, Gran," Kelly replied, kissing her grandmother's cheek. Now that the truth was out, she felt a strange peace filling her. "I need to talk to James."

"This way, ladies," George said, sweeping his arm in the direction of the door. "Sorry, James, if we caused difficulties," he added as Elizabeth and Mary preceded him.

"No problem, George. Just keep those two occupied until after breakfast tomorrow."

It wasn't going to take that long to explain to James, Kelly realized, but she'd worry about where she'd spend the night later.

He closed the door and then leaned against it.

"Why didn't you tell me?"

She met his gaze, in spite of the tremors that shook her. Then she sank back to the couch and looked away. "I was in shock. We'd just married this morning because we both thought I was pregnant.'' In a rush, she added, pleading with her eyes as she looked at him again, ''I promise it wasn't a trick, James. I believed I was pregnant as much as you did.''

He stepped away from the door. ''I know that.'' Reaching the couch, he sat down beside her, his arm extending behind her shoulders.

His closeness made her nervous. The urge to dive into his arms, to feel them around her, his lips on hers, was almost more than she could control. But she didn't have that right.

''I think you can get the marriage annulled fairly easily since we haven't slept with each other. I was going to tell you before—before things could go any further.'' She shifted away from him slightly, trying to remain strong.

''But you're wrong.''

Her gaze whipped back to him in surprise. ''No, James, I'm sure an annulment will be fairly easy.''

''We have slept together.''

She stared up at him in confusion. ''No, we haven't.'' She would've remembered if they'd consummated their marriage, since it was exactly what she wanted.

''Then how could we think you were pregnant?''

''We haven't since the marriage ceremony,'' she corrected herself, irritated with him for being so obtuse.

''I think we can rectify that,'' he murmured and, before she realized what he was doing, scooped her up from the sofa and headed toward the bedroom.

"James! What are you doing?"

"Making sure an annulment isn't possible."

"But, James, I'm not pregnant. You don't have to be trapped into marriage for the sake of the baby."

He lay her down on the bed and quickly sank down beside her, taking her hand in his. "You know, when you first asked me to be the father of your child, I said no."

She nodded, wondering what he was trying to say.

"I said that wasn't a good enough reason. Remember?"

She nodded again, tears filling her eyes. No, it wasn't. As much as she mourned the loss of the child she never had, she was relieved that James didn't have to be held by a marriage for that reason. She knew now that there was only one reason to share the birth of a child, a marriage, a life together. And if James didn't feel that reason, then, as miserable as she would be, she would be better off alone.

"Well, I've found the right reason to be the father of your child, and nothing is going to change my mind."

"Wh-what reason?" she whispered, her throat tight with the suddenly rising hope that he felt as she did. That, against all the odds, he loved her as she loved him.

"The reason I intend to be the father of any child you have is because I love you with all my heart. I want you by my side every minute of my life."

"James, are you sure?" How badly she wanted to believe him. If he loved her—

He stretched out beside her, wrapping his arms around her again. "I'm more than sure. But you haven't said anything. Your grandmother's well. You don't have to do anything drastic to save her life. You're not pregnant. You're free to go or do whatever you want."

"Oh, James, I've loved you for so long. I can't think of another place I'd rather be than here with you." She buried her face in his neck, seeking his warmth, his strength. When his arms tightened around her, she felt as if she'd come home. A home that she'd longed for with all her heart.

"Then for your grandmother's sake, and any child we might make, it's a good thing we got married this morning, 'cause I don't intend to let you out of this bed for a long, long time."

"You'll get no argument from me," she assured him as her lips eagerly met his.

She'd found the perfect father for her child. But more importantly, she'd found the love of her life, a love like Granddad and Gran had shared. A love she would hold in her heart for the rest of her life.

Epilogue

"Hi, Gran, Mary. Where's Kelly?"

Kelly smiled as she heard James's cheerful greeting. He'd agreed to move into Gran's home without any complaints. The four of them, with Blondie, had become a family. The dog's excited barks accompanied the sound of footsteps on the stairs.

"Kelly, I'm home!"

His voice preceded him, but she didn't move. Seated on the bed, she had five packages lined up before her.

Their bedroom door opened, and James came to an abrupt halt. "What are you doing?"

"I'm getting ready to take a test. Want to help me?"

He moved over beside her and picked up the first package. "Uh-huh." He replaced it and picked up the second, the third, the fourth and then the last one. "Do you really think all of these are necessary?"

"I'm not taking any chances. Dr. Jerrell said we should try several different tests and go with the majority." She grinned up at her husband of three months. The most glorious three months she'd ever shared.

"Well, since I participated in what prompted these tests, I think it's only right that I participate in the tests themselves," he assured her, giving her a smacking kiss on the lips. "And if you're not pregnant, Kelly, my love, I guess we'll just have to keep practicing." His voice had sunk to a whisper as he finished and his lips covered hers in a kiss that brought all thought to a halt in Kelly's head.

He could always do that to her. And she didn't think it would ever change, even when they reached Gran's age.

He released her and picked up the first one. As he read the directions, he said, "By the way, Mom called today from Phoenix. She wanted to tell me again how much they loved you. They asked when we'd be out for another visit."

"Mmm, that depends on the tests, I think."

"Well, let's get started, Madam Townsend."

Ten minutes later, they stood locked in an embrace, watching for the results of the test. One by one, all five tests showed the same result.

James whooped with excited laughter before picking Kelly up and spinning around. "We're going to be parents, sweetheart!"

"For the baby's sake, I hope the two downstairs and your parents are a little calmer than you," she teased, delight in her smile.

"For the baby's sake," James assured her, "you'd better hope we have three or four. Otherwise, this little tyke will be mighty spoiled."

"No," she assured him, kissing him, "our baby won't be spoiled too much, because we're giving our baby the best gift of all—love."

"You're right," he agreed, "and we've got plenty of that to go around, no matter how many babies we have."

He tightened their embrace, his lips settling on hers. Later, they'd tell Gran and Mary their wonderful news, and then they'd call his parents in Phoenix.

But not yet. They had some personal celebrating to do first.

COMING NEXT MONTH

#557 ONCE UPON A HONEYMOON by Julie Kistler
Self-proclaimed bachelor Tripp Ashby was in a no-win situation...and only
Bridget Emerick could help him. His old pal had bailed him out since college—but
this time, the sexy bachelor needed the unthinkable...a wife! *Don't miss the second
book in the STUDS miniseries!*

#558 QUINN'S WAY by Rebecca Flanders
Heartbeat
When David Quinn appeared out of nowhere and entered Houston Malloy's ordered
life—mouthwatering smile, bedroom eyes and all—she thought the man was out of
this world. Little did she know how right she was!

#559 SECRET AGENT DAD by Leandra Logan
As a secret agent, Michael Hawkes had stared down danger with nerves of steel. But
then he found himself protecting his old flame Valerie Warner—and her twins—in
the jungles of suburbia. Twins who looked an awful lot like him.... Michael never saw
danger like he did now!

#560 FROM DRIFTER TO DADDY by Mollie Molay
Rising Star
For a couple of hundred bucks Sara Martin bought the wrongfully imprisoned drifter
Quinn Tucker for thirty days. But it didn't take long for Quinn to know he was safer
in jail, doing his time, than he was out on a ranch with a gorgeous woman and her
ready-made family....

AVAILABLE THIS MONTH:

MILLION DOLLAR SWEEPSTAKES (III)

No purchase necessary. To enter the sweepstakes and receive the Free Books and Surprise Gift, follow the directions published and complete and mail your "Win A Fortune" Game Card. If not taking advantage of the book and gift offer or if the "Win A Fortune" Game Card is missing, you may enter by hand-printing your name and address on a 3" X 5" card and mailing it (limit: one entry per envelope) via First Class Mail to: Million Dollar Sweepstakes (III) "Win A Fortune" Game, P.O. Box 1867, Buffalo, NY 14269-1867, or Million Dollar Sweepstakes (III) "Win A Fortune" Game, P.O. Box 609, Fort Erie, Ontario L2A 5X3. When your entry is received, you will be assigned sweepstakes numbers. To be eligible entries must be received no later than March 31, 1996. No liability is assumed for printing errors or lost, late or misdirected entries. Odds of winning are determined by the number of eligible entries distributed and received.

Sweepstakes open to residents of the U.S. (except Puerto Rico), Canada, Europe and Taiwan who are 18 years of age or older. All applicable laws and regulations apply. Sweepstakes offer void wherever prohibited by law. Values of all prizes are in U.S. currency. This sweepstakes is presented by Torstar Corp, its subsidiaries and affiliates, in conjunction with book, merchandise and/or product offerings. For a copy of the official rules governing this sweepstakes offer, send a self-addressed, stamped envelope (WA residents need not affix return postage) to: MILLION DOLLAR SWEEPSTAKES (III) Rules, P.O. Box 4573, Blair, NE 68009, USA.

SWP-H994

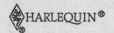 HARLEQUIN®

SUNDAYS ON CBS HARLEQUIN™ MOVIES WATCH FOR THEM!

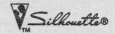 Silhouette®

The movie event of the season can be the reading event of the year!

Lights… The lights go on in October when CBS presents Harlequin/Silhouette Sunday Matinee Movies. These four movies are based on bestselling Harlequin and Silhouette novels.

Camera… As the cameras roll, be the first to read the original novels the movies are based on!

Action… Through this offer, you can have these books sent directly to you! Just fill in the order form below and you could be reading the books…before the movie!

48288-4	Treacherous Beauties by Cheryl Emerson		
	$3.99 U.S./$4.50 CAN.	☐
83305-9	Fantasy Man by Sharon Green		
	$3.99 U.S./$4.50 CAN.	☐
48289-2	A Change of Place by Tracy Sinclair		
	$3.99 U.S./$4.50CAN.	☐
83306-7	Another Woman by Margot Dalton		
	$3.99 U.S./$4.50 CAN.	☐

TOTAL AMOUNT $
POSTAGE & HANDLING $
(\$1.00 for one book, 50¢ for each additional)
APPLICABLE TAXES* $ _____
TOTAL PAYABLE $ _____
(check or money order—please do not send cash)

To order, complete this form and send it, along with a check or money order for the total above, payable to Harlequin Books, to: **In the U.S.:** 3010 Walden Avenue, P.O. Box 9047, Buffalo, NY 14269-9047; **In Canada:** P.O. Box 613, Fort Erie, Ontario, L2A 5X3.

Name: _____

Address: _____ City: _____

State/Prov.: _____ Zip/Postal Code: _____

*New York residents remit applicable sales taxes.
  Canadian residents remit applicable GST and provincial taxes.

CBSPR

"HOORAY FOR HOLLYWOOD" SWEEPSTAKES

HERE'S HOW THE SWEEPSTAKES WORKS

OFFICIAL RULES — NO PURCHASE NECESSARY

To enter, complete an Official Entry Form or hand print on a 3" x 5" card the words "HOORAY FOR HOLLYWOOD", your name and address and mail your entry in the pre-addressed envelope (if provided) or to: "Hooray for Hollywood" Sweepstakes, P.O. Box 9076, Buffalo, NY 14269-9076 or "Hooray for Hollywood" Sweepstakes, P.O. Box 637, Fort Erie, Ontario L2A 5X3. Entries must be sent via First Class Mail and be received no later than 12/31/94. No liability is assumed for lost, late or misdirected mail.

Winners will be selected in random drawings to be conducted no later than January 31, 1995 from all eligible entries received.

Grand Prize: A 7-day/6-night trip for 2 to Los Angeles, CA including round trip air transportation from commercial airport nearest winner's residence, accommodations at the Regent Beverly Wilshire Hotel, free rental car, and $1,000 spending money. (Approximate prize value which will vary dependent upon winner's residence: $5,400.00 U.S.); 500 Second Prizes: A pair of "Hollywood Star" sunglasses (prize value: $9.95 U.S. each). Winner selection is under the supervision of D.L. Blair, Inc., an independent judging organization, whose decisions are final. Grand Prize travelers must sign and return a release of liability prior to traveling. Trip must be taken by 2/1/96 and is subject to airline schedules and accommodations availability.

Sweepstakes offer is open to residents of the U.S. (except Puerto Rico) and Canada who are 18 years of age or older, except employees and immediate family members of Harlequin Enterprises, Ltd., its affiliates, subsidiaries, and all agencies, entities or persons connected with the use, marketing or conduct of this sweepstakes. All federal, state, provincial, municipal and local laws apply. Offer void wherever prohibited by law. Taxes and/or duties are the sole responsibility of the winners. Any litigation within the province of Quebec respecting the conduct and awarding of prizes may be submitted to the Regie des loteries et courses du Quebec. All prizes will be awarded; winners will be notified by mail. No substitution of prizes are permitted. Odds of winning are dependent upon the number of eligible entries received.

Potential grand prize winner must sign and return an Affidavit of Eligibility within 30 days of notification. In the event of non-compliance within this time period, prize may be awarded to an alternate winner. Prize notification returned as undeliverable may result in the awarding of prize to an alternate winner. By acceptance of their prize, winners consent to use of their names, photographs, or likenesses for purpose of advertising, trade and promotion on behalf of Harlequin Enterprises, Ltd., without further compensation unless prohibited by law. A Canadian winner must correctly answer an arithmetical skill-testing question in order to be awarded the prize.

For a list of winners (available after 2/28/95), send a separate stamped, self-addressed envelope to: Hooray for Hollywood Sweepstakes 3252 Winners, P.O. Box 4200, Blair, NE 68009.

CBSRLS

OFFICIAL ENTRY COUPON

"Hooray for Hollywood"
SWEEPSTAKES!

Yes, I'd love to win the Grand Prize — a vacation in Hollywood —
or one of 500 pairs of "sunglasses of the stars"! Please enter me
in the sweepstakes!

This entry must be received by December 31, 1994.
Winners will be notified by January 31, 1995.

Name _____

Address _____ Apt. _____

City _____

State/Prov. _____ Zip/Postal Code _____

Daytime phone number _____
                              (area code)

Mail all entries to: Hooray for Hollywood Sweepstakes,
P.O. Box 9076, Buffalo, NY 14269-9076.
In Canada, mail to: Hooray for Hollywood Sweepstakes,
P.O. Box 637, Fort Erie, ON L2A 5X3.

KCH

OFFICIAL ENTRY COUPON

"Hooray for Hollywood"
SWEEPSTAKES!

Yes, I'd love to win the Grand Prize — a vacation in Hollywood —
or one of 500 pairs of "sunglasses of the stars"! Please enter me
in the sweepstakes!

This entry must be received by December 31, 1994.
Winners will be notified by January 31, 1995.

Name _____

Address _____ Apt. _____

City _____

State/Prov. _____ Zip/Postal Code _____

Daytime phone number _____
                              (area code)

Mail all entries to: Hooray for Hollywood Sweepstakes,
P.O. Box 9076, Buffalo, NY 14269-9076.
In Canada, mail to: Hooray for Hollywood Sweepstakes,
P.O. Box 637, Fort Erie, ON L2A 5X3.

KCH